W9-AMN-484

COVERUP

COVERUP

A NOVEL

JAY BENNETT

Learning Resources Center
Jordan High School
Jordan, Minnesota

FRANKLIN WATTS
NEW YORK LONDON TORONTO SYDNEY
1991

40443

Library of Congress Cataloging-in-Publication Data
Bennett, Jay.
Coverup / by Jay Bennett.
p.   cm.
Summary: Teenage Brad is tormented by confused memories of a drunken
ride with his best friend Alden, during which they may
have hit and killed a man.
ISBN 0-531-11091-5. — ISBN 0-531-15224-3
[1. Mystery and detective stories.] I. Title.
PZ7.B4399Co   1991
[Fic]—dc20   91-18506   CIP   AC

Copyright © 1991 by Jay Bennett
All rights reserved
Printed in the United States of America
5   4   3   2   1

For
Ceyenna and Katie

COVERUP

1

He awoke in a cold sweat, pale and trembling, his eyes wildly trying to pierce the black night.

He shivered.

Then he called out, in a tight, small voice.

"Alden."

There was no answering sound.

Only silence. The dread silence of the night.

He trembled again and then he got out of bed and went softly out of the dark room and down the carpeted hall, his bare feet glimmering.

He was alone in the empty house.

His parents were in Hawaii. Thousands of miles away. On vacation. And he was alone. Alone in the vast empty house.

He went slowly down the shadowy stairway and into the kitchen.

He felt nauseous.

He had drunk too much at the party with Alden. Too much.

He went to the gas range and turned on the burner under the coffeepot.

Then he sat down on a chair and waited in the silvery darkness, his pale hands trembling.

And he said to himself, what happened?

Did I dream it?

Or did something happen?

Something terrible and deadly.

"Alden."

And as he listened to his voice fade into the cold stillness, he felt so alone.

So desperately alone.

And terrified.

What had happened?

2

He remembered as through a shimmering mist.

The party.

The blurred voices.

The blaring music.

The drinking.

Yes, the drinking.

Then . . .

"Brad?"

He turned and saw Alden standing at his side.

"Yes?" he said.

"Let's split, Brad."

"Why?"

"The party's getting dead." Alden was swaying.

"Where's Marian?" Brad asked.

"No."

"She came here with us."

"No."

"So we're taking her home with us."

Alden put his hand on Brad's shoulder and shook his head. "Are you my friend?" he asked.

"Been that since we were kids in this town," Brad said.

"Good."

"So?"

Alden leaned his handsome face close to Brad's and whispered, "Then be my friend and let's knock it off."

"Had a fight with her?"

"Uh-huh."

"You always have a fight when you drink too much," Brad said.

"So?"

"So go back and make up with her."

"No," Alden said.

"You'll only do it tomorrow."

"I won't."

"Alden."

"No. Let's go."

"Maybe I'll stay here a little while longer," Brad said.

"Why?"

"I'm a little shaky. Maybe some coffee will settle me down."

"No."

"I'll grab a ride."

Alden shook his head decisively. "You came with me, you go with me."

"You shouldn't drive," Brad said.

"Why not?"

"Too much in you."

"Okay. So you drive my car."

"I'm just as bad as you, Alden. I'm groggy. I'll fall asleep at the wheel."

"You won't."

"Let's ask Eliot. He's always in good shape," Brad said.

"Eliot?"

"Why not? He'll be glad to do it."

"I don't like him," Alden said.

"Stop it. He's one of your best friends."

Alden leaned close to Brad. There were beads of sweat on his forehead. "You're my best friend," he said.

"So is Eliot."

Alden waved his hand angrily. "You're my best friend. The best. The top. Only you, Brad."

"Let's get hold of Eliot."

"Still with him?"

"Still."

"Eliot."

"Eliot."

Alden suddenly laughed. "We sound like a vaudeville team."

"Let's get him," Brad said quietly.

Alden stood there swaying and considering and then came to a decision. "It's my car, isn't it?" he said.

"Sure. But . . ."

"My car. I'll drive."

Brad shook his head. "Let's stay here a while, Buddy."

"No. It's my car," Alden insisted.

"Just a while. I'm not up to it."

"We're going."

"Alden."

"I said, let's go."

And he saw the commanding look come into Alden's eyes, and heard the harsh, low voice. "Brad."

Alden could be a mean drunk if he didn't have his way.

Brad remembered how he had silently followed Alden out into the summer night. And remembered the car's doors slamming shut, one after the other.

Like the iron doors of prison cells.

One after the other.

3

Alden was singing.

He remembered that, remembered it vividly. And the words of the song. Alden always sang it when he was high.

"My name is Yon Yonson
I live in Wisconsin
I work in the lumber yard there
I walk on the street
And the people I meet
They ask me what is your name?
And I tell them
My name is Yon Yonson
I live in Wisconsin
I work in the lumber yard there
I walk on the street
And the people I meet
They ask me what is your name?

And I tell them
My name is Yon ..."

And Brad remembered his eyes closing to the interminable song and when he opened them again, they were riding along the beach road and there were lacy whitecaps far out on the Sound. The moon lay full and bright on the broad dark water. The night breeze was soft and gentle, cooling his feverish face.

Suddenly Alden drove the car off the road and onto the beach. The sand sprayed up around them. The car stopped abruptly and Alden swung about to Brad, a mad light in his eyes.

"Let's go for a swim," he said.

"What?"

"Come on. We'll skinny dip."

Brad shook his head. "I'm not up to it."

"Come on. It'll clear your head," Alden said.

"No. I'll only get sick and—"

"So what?"

"Take me home, Alden. I want to get into a bed. Please."

"I'm swimming."

Alden got out of the car and took off his clothes and then ran naked into the water. His body gleamed in the moonlight. Brad watched him splash about and then his eyes started to close again. He heard Alden's shouting voice as if in a dream.

"Brad."

He slowly opened his eyes again.

"Come on in. It's great. Sober you up."

"No, Alden," he murmured.

Alden started to sing.

"My name is Yon Yonson
I come from Wisconsin

I work in the lumber yard there . . ."

Alden's voice floated in from the water.

Far out were the whitecaps. Glistening, fading, and then glistening again. White, lacy strips of foam. Far, far out.

"My name is Yon Yonson
I come from Wisconsin
I work . . ."

Brad listened and thought lazily, you're getting the words wrong, Alden. It's "I live in Wisconsin," not "come from Wisconsin," the words, the words, Alden, and then the voice and the words slowly faded away and his eyes closed again.

He slept.

When he opened his eyes again, the car was moving down Wilson Lane. He lazily wondered why.

He looked over at Alden. He saw that Alden's blond hair was wet and there were trickles of water on his clear, determined chin.

Alden grinned at him. "How're you doing, buddy?"

"Not good, Alden."

Alden laughed. "Go back to sleep. I'm taking the back road. You'll be home soon."

"Okay."

"Sleep, old buddy."

"Sure."

But he didn't sleep. He leaned back against the leather seat and thought of Alden Whitlock, son of Judge Peter Whitlock. There had been Whitlocks in Elmont since before the Revolution. Four of them had been governors of the state. And Alden was now being groomed to become the next in line.

Brilliant Alden Whitlock. Brilliant, handsome,

and personable. Great adjectives to use later on. High school valedictorian.

Going to Yale University in the fall. All the Whitlocks had gone to Yale.

You're going to make it, Brad thought. It's all there waiting for you. Step by step. All being carefully prepared. No chance of messing up.

And I'm glad for you. You're a good and decent fellow. My best friend. Always have been.

He remembered with a warm glow when Alden passed him the baton on the last lap in the Penn Relays. The last quarter of a mile. He took the baton, held it tight, and then ran his heart out to win the championship for the team.

Breaking the record.

Alden and the rest of the team hugging him while the crowd roared.

Brad laughed softly, still hearing the crowd noise, and then it all slowly faded and his eyes gently closed again.

And it was then he thought it had happened. While he was dreaming of the Penn Relays. And Alden passing him the baton. Their hands touching in friendship.

It was then.

A soft thud and the car stopping abruptly and then the sound of the car door opening and shutting. A sharp, metallic sound that pierced the night. On lonely, deserted Wilson Lane.

They had stopped just by an old oak tree that had been gutted by lightning. Through the slits of his half-opened eyes Brad could see the bare, gnarled branches of the dead tree and then Alden stooping in front of the car, the headlights streaming their cold rays over his face. A white, tense face. Mouth dropping open.

18

And then the darkness flowed into the slits of the eyes and he was sleeping again.

This time it was a heavy, drunken sleep.

And in his sleep he saw again the gnarled branches of the oak tree. They were like two desperate arms raised in fury against the black night. He could almost hear mingled voices, crying out in terror, while the two desperate arms shook violently.

Shook.

Shook.

Then someone was shaking him and he was dimly awake.

Alden was standing in the moonlit darkness, holding the door open.

Brad's house loomed up before him, dark and vague.

Alden stood straight and tall, no longer swaying. A thin smile spread over his white face.

"You're home, Brad."

"Oh."

"Want to sleep in the car or get up to bed?" And he laughed.

"Help me out, Alden."

"Sure, buddy."

Alden put the key in the lock for him and then opened the house door.

"You'll be all right, Brad?" he asked.

"I hope so."

"Want me to help you upstairs?"

Brad shook his head. "I'll make it."

Alden patted him on the shoulder and turned to leave. "See you in the morning."

"It's almost morning now."

"That's right, Brad. It is."

He was standing by the softly gleaming white car.

Brad leaned against the door jamb, swaying just a bit.

They stood looking at each other, in silence.

Far in the distance, a dog barked. A lonely, mournful sound. Then the sound was gone and the stillness of the vast night washed over them again.

"Alden?"

"Yes?"

Brad opened his lips but he didn't say anything.

Then Alden spoke again, his voice low and soft, his blue eyes clear and penetrating.

"What is it?"

Brad slowly shook his head. "Nothing, Alden. Nothing."

"You sure?" The eyes were still penetrating.

"I'm sure."

But deep down there was something he wanted to ask.

Deep down in the forest of his being, something had stirred. Something that sent thrills of vague fear through him. But it was too deep down. He said nothing.

"So long, buddy," Alden said.

"So long."

He stood in the doorway, swaying unsteadily, as he watched Alden drive off into the night.

Then he closed the door.

4

Brad sat on the chair in the kitchen watching the steady blue flame of the gas jet.

He could see once again Alden's clear and penetrating blue eyes, staring through the night at him. Staring and probing.

Probing for what, Alden? Did something happen? Did it?

He sighed and turned off the flame.

He drank as much coffee as he could without retching and then he dragged himself up the staircase, past his parents' empty moonlit room and into his own.

He flopped down on his bed and instantly fell asleep. A deep, undisturbed sleep, as though he had been drugged.

The sound of the telephone woke him.

He opened his eyes and saw sunlight streaming

into the room. The white shade on one of the windows rustled softly in the early afternoon breeze.

Brad listened to the cold ring of the telephone coming from downstairs. He didn't move. Just lay there, looking at the rustling shade.

The ringing stopped.

Only the rustling remained.

But the terror that had waked him during the night now slowly and quietly seeped back into him.

Then the phone rang again. Long and persistent. This time it wouldn't stop.

Brad muttered a curse. He slowly got out of bed and went down the stairs into the hallway and picked up the receiver. It was cold to his hand. His shadow lay dark against the sunlit wall. His voice sounded distant to him when he spoke. Distant and fearful.

"Hello?"

"Brad?"

It was Alden.

"Yes?"

"Just get up?"

"You got me up," Brad said curtly.

"How do you feel?"

"Lousy."

Alden laughed. He was in good spirits. "You'll be okay," he said. "Just take a cold shower and sing."

"No."

"Don't forget to sing. Yon Yonson."

"I'm going back to bed," Brad said.

"Forget it. We're going swimming."

"No, Alden."

"Over at Marian's. She's having a pool party."

"You talking to her again?" Brad asked.

"Sure. You said we would. Everything's fine."

"Oh."

"You remember saying that to me? Don't you?"

"Yes, Alden," Brad said, looking at his dark shadow on the wall.

"Come on, Brad. Take your shower and drive over."

"I don't think so."

"Come on, old buddy. We had a great time in the water last night. Didn't we?"

"In the water? What water?" Brad asked.

Alden laughed.

"Stop conning me, Alden," Brad said.

"I'm not. Don't you remember?"

"Remember what?"

"On the way home. We stopped on the beach and then went in swimming," Alden said.

Brad was silent.

He heard Alden's voice again.

"You started to swim far out and I had to shout to you to come back."

"Alden," he said softly.

"You wanted to swim all the way to Long Island. That's what you said. Don't you remember?"

"No."

"It's all a blank to you?" Alden asked.

"I guess it is."

"Can't be. I don't believe it."

"I remember nothing, Alden," he said.

There was a silence. Then he heard Alden's voice again. "If you change your mind, come on over to Marian's."

"Sure."

"Be seeing you, Brad."

But Alden didn't hang up.

There was a pause. And then Alden's voice again. "So you remember nothing?"

"Nothing, Alden."

I remember sitting in the car and watching you swim, Alden. I remember that.

Alden's voice came through to him. "After the swim we ran up and down the beach drying out and you were singing Yon Yonson with me. Then we got back in the car. And you fell asleep. You conked out."

"I remember falling asleep," Brad said slowly.

"But not going into the water?"

"Not that."

"Strange. When I left you at the door you said, 'It was a great swim, Alden.' And then you said, 'Let's drive back and have another.' And we both started to laugh."

"It's a blank," Brad murmured. "A complete blank."

"So it's a blank. Means nothing. Come on over to the pool."

"Maybe."

"So long, Brad."

"Wait," Brad suddenly said.

"What is it?"

Brad paused and then spoke. "Alden, how did you take me home last night?"

"What do you mean?"

"What road?"

"The same way we always do. The—"

Brad cut in. "You didn't go down Wilson Lane?"

"What?"

"Did you?"

"Why should I? It's out of the way," Alden said.

"You certain?"

"Of course I am."

"Alden, I have to know."

"And I'm telling you."

"Don't jerk me around. The truth, Alden."

Alden's voice tightened when he spoke. "Listen, Brad. I know I was high last night. But not that high. We were nowhere near Wilson Lane. You stop jerking yourself around."

Brad stood there in silence.

And then he heard Alden's voice again. "Come on over to Marian's."

He didn't speak.

"Brad?"

"I'm here."

"Take that shower," Alden said.

"I guess I will."

"You need it, old buddy. You're flying."

And then he heard the click.

He was alone again, alone in the silent, empty house, his shadow dark on the white shining wall. His hand still gripped the black receiver.

He could hear the window shade upstairs.

The wind had risen and the shade was no longer rustling.

It was flapping now, flapping in the vast and eerie silence. Flapping sharply against the window, with a ceaseless rhythm.

He stood motionless, listening to the sound.

And he heard Alden's voice again.

We were not on Wilson Lane.

No, Brad.

Nowhere near Wilson Lane.

Nowhere.

Nowhere.

The voice whispered away into the stillness.

He stood motionless, and in the forest of his being, terror like a black panther moved between the trees. A panther with glowing eyes.

He shivered.
His lips trembled.
But no words came through.
Yet he spoke within himself.
Something had happened, he said.
Something terrible.
I know it did.
And I feel that my life will never be the same again.
Never.

5

He was lying on a chaise near the edge of the pool, alone, a bit away from the others. He glanced over at his friends. Some of them were swimming. Others were just sitting around the glistening white tables, talking and laughing.

Marian walked over and sat down beside him. "What's the matter, Brad?"

He looked over at her. She was of medium height, with long dark hair and hazel eyes. Her eyes were always smiling. And yet behind them he felt there was a searching, a sad searching for something that was always beyond her reach.

You have everything, Marian, he thought to himself. What is it you really want?

He heard her voice. "Tell me, Brad," she said.

"What do you mean?"

"You don't seem to be with us today."

"I guess I'm not," he said.

"What's wrong?"

"A hangover. Too much to drink last night."

She shook her head.

Someone at the other side of the pool called to her and she laughed and waved her hand. It flashed in the rich sun.

"It's not that," she said to Brad.

"What then?"

She played with his brown, curly hair.

"Something else," she said.

He smiled and said nothing. You like me, Marian, he said to himself. And that's as far as you'll let it go. You've made your choice with Alden.

"You seem to be brooding over something, Brad."

"Do I? Just a hangover, Marian. Nothing more."

"Tell me."

He looked away from her and over to the diving board. Alden stood poised in the late afternoon sun, ready to dive. He stood tall against the darkening sky, tall and blond and statuesque. His face was calm and concentrated.

"He has it, doesn't he," Marian said quietly. "Did you ever know?" she continued.

"Know what?" Brad asked.

"That you're a very good looking fellow? If I chucked Alden is there any chance that you would go for me?"

He smiled. "Like a shot, Marian."

But he knew he never would. She was a good friend and that was as far as it went.

"That's good to know, Brad."

He laughed. "You're not chucking Alden. And he's not chucking you," he said.

28

She smiled softly. Then she looked away from him to Alden.

"Marian," Brad said.

"Yes?"

"How did you go home last night?"

"Oh. Eliot borrowed a car and drove me." She turned back to him and started to laugh.

He looked at her questioningly.

"We stopped for a minute to watch you and Alden swim."

"What?"

"Just for a minute."

He sat up slowly. "You saw me swimming?" he said.

She nodded. "You were way out and Alden was shouting at you."

A cold thrill went through him. "And then what?"

"We drove on. I was still angry at Alden."

Brad didn't speak.

Marian laughed again. "It was funny seeing the two of you skinny-dipping out there in the middle of the night and no one around but the sky and the sand."

"The two of us," Brad said in a low voice.

"The two of us," Alden said. He had emerged from the pool and was now standing near them, smiling at Brad.

"Still don't remember?" Alden said.

Brad didn't answer.

"You had a bad night, old buddy," Alden said gently.

He picked up a towel and started drying himself.

Marian sat there silently, watching the two of them. Brad thought he saw a sad look come into her eyes. But then it was gone.

Alden flung the towel onto one of the beach chairs and came closer to Brad. "But we had a good time at the party, didn't we?" he said.

Brad nodded. "We did, Alden."

"A lot of fun. Right?"

"Yes."

Alden's penetrating blue eyes were on Brad. He grinned. "And that's all that matters, isn't it?"

"That's all that matters, Alden."

"They call us the fun generation, don't they?"

Brad didn't speak.

"Instant gratification," Marian said and laughed softly.

"That's what they say about us," Brad murmured.

"So we have fun," Alden smiled. "And what's wrong in that? Just look around you. Isn't everybody enjoying themselves?"

"They are," Brad said. But he kept looking at Alden.

There was a silence.

Marian suddenly got up. "It's time to go in and eat," she said.

"Come on, Brad," Alden smiled.

Brad didn't move.

Marian turned away from them. She called out in a loud, cheery voice to the people who sat in clusters around the huge, Olympic-size pool. "We're going inside now. Chow time. Chow time."

"I'll lie out here awhile, Alden," Brad said.

"Not hungry?"

"Not yet."

"Your stomach okay?"

"Yes."

"Then you'll come in?"

Brad nodded. "Later."

30

Alden reached down and mussed his hair. "Stop brooding. Lighten up, old buddy. Lighten up."

"It's fun time," Brad said softly.

"It's fun time."

Then he watched Alden and the rest of his friends saunter into the large, white rambling house.

He lay there alone and a chill came over him, although the evening was warm and close, like most midsummer evenings. He reached over and picked up a heavy beach towel and then covered himself with it. The chill would not leave him.

A stillness settled over the pool. The water rippled quietly as the soft tint of the dying sun spread gently over it like a shimmering veil. Shimmering and red.

He thought of blood and wondered why the image had come into his mind.

The water rippled.

He lay on the chaise until darkness swept down and enveloped him. Lay there, motionless, his brooding eyes staring into the evening.

From inside, he could hear the muted laughing of his friends.

The fun generation.

He listened.

Finally, he slowly got up and went into the house and joined them.

Soon he was laughing, too.

6

During the night, Brad awoke. He was cold and trembling violently. He had not been dreaming. Just woke up from a deep, peaceful, and healing sleep. Suddenly. As though someone had brutally jerked him awake.

He sat up in bed staring into the darkness.

"We were on Wilson Lane," he whispered.

We were. And I saw Alden kneeling in front of the headlights. I did.

I heard a thud. A soft thud. As if we had hit something.

Alden's face was pale. And his mouth was open. Open as though he were screaming.

A thud.

A soft thud.

I know it happened.

I do.

"I do," he whispered. His voice rustled away into the darkness.

Then he got out of bed and quickly dressed.

He went down the stairs and out of the house and into the car. The car door slammed shut, shattering the stillness of the night.

He sat there rigid before turning on the motor. His thoughts were swirling about. And then they centered on one image.

The tree.

I must find the tree.

The lightning-blasted dead tree that stood on the side of the road.

I must see it again.

Then I will know.

I will.

7

Brad drove somberly through the silent night until he came to the turnoff for Wilson Lane. The moon hung in the black, endless sky, casting a thin, wavery gleam over the narrow road. The windows of the few solitary wooden houses were dark. Dark and glinting. Beyond the houses, grassy fields stretched wide and treeless. Nothing living was about. Nothing moved. It was so desolate. All so desolate and lost.

Brad listened to the mournful sound of the tires as they spun over the empty, winding road.

Was I here last night? Was I?

Why did I drink so much? Why do we all drink so much? What are we trying to prove? What are we trying to find?

It's like being on this road. You end up in a dark, desolate night. With fears and terrors. And doubts.

Was I here last night?

Was I?

I don't know.

I'll never know.

Brad listened to the relentless sound of the tires and stared into the starless night ahead of him. Suddenly he heard the piercing scream of a cat far ahead of him and then it slowly died away. He listened and then slowed the car down.

What am I doing here? he suddenly asked himself. This is madness. I could be wrong. Badly wrong.

This is an old back road and always has been. Never changed. No one ever uses it. No one. Only the few people who still live in these old, stray houses. They're like hermits here. In a world all their own.

Then why do I think that Alden would ever come down this road?

Why?

It doesn't make any sense.

You're a jerk, Brad. Give it up and go back home and get to bed again. Forget last night. You were drunk, so forget it.

I can't remember.

I can't.

I do remember being here many years ago. When I was a small child. My father was looking for a fishing pond he had heard of. Great for perch, Brad. We'll have a fine time fishing, son. Fishing together. Just you and I.

The tires spun around and around.

If I could only get back there again, Brad thought. We were very close then, my father and I. It was such a good time of life. And then subtly, very subtly, we drifted apart. Why?

Give it up.

Brad stopped the car and sat there thinking. The

moonlight glinted over the wide, lonely fields. Again he heard the scream of the cat, and this time it sounded like a death scream.

Suddenly Brad nodded his head.

"Yes," he whispered.

He nodded his head slowly again. A strange look in his eyes. He laughed softly.

"That's it," he whispered.

Doesn't make sense that Alden would come down this road? Doesn't? Brad laughed again.

When you're drunk nothing makes sense, he said to himself. Isn't that so?

He started the car again and drove on down the lonely road, the strange, almost mad look still in his eyes.

Alden came here because he was still high. Even after the swim. He was still very drunk. He must've missed the turnoff to my house and then went on down the highway for miles, still singing Yon Yonson, and he suddenly saw Wilson Lane come up and he decided to go through it. The long way to my house.

Alden was here all right. Because he was drunk.

Brad grinned and drove on.

But then he suddenly slowed down, his face tight and thoughtful again.

Drunk?

But so was I. Even worse than Alden. I was out of it most of the time. Asleep. And when I wasn't, I was in a drunken haze.

I don't remember what really happened.

Swimming?

They claim I went in swimming with Alden. That's what Marian and Alden say. Skinny-dipping? I don't remember getting out of the car. And then I ran on the beach with him?

36

Marian saw us.

Why should she lie to me? What reason?

I remember nothing. It's all a blank. Like it never happened. The whole night.

Maybe we were never on Wilson Lane. Maybe I'm just imagining it all. Why not?

The whole night is a blur to me. I was drunk. Drunk. I should turn around and go back to the house and forget it all. It was all a drunken dream. That's what it was. That's what it is. Nothing but a drunken—

Brad suddenly hit the brake hard and the car stopped abruptly. He left the motor running, the head-lights on, and jumped out of the car. Then he stood stock-still and gasped.

"No. It can't be."

His voice was low and hoarse.

For there on the side of the desolate road, stand-ing alone, completely alone, was the tree. The lightning-blasted tree, its gnarled branches, like black twisted arms, raised bitterly against the dark sky. He stared at the tree and shivered.

This is the spot, he said to himself. The exact spot. I didn't imagine it. I didn't.

Here is the tree.

And here is where it happened.

In his feverish mind, he again heard the thud. The soft deadly thud. He winced as if in pain.

Through the slits of his half-closed eyes, as in a dream, he saw Alden kneeling in front of the white, shining car. Tiny bits of headlight glass were gleaming in his hand. Alden's eyes were staring, as if into death. His mouth dropping open. His face pale. Glints of sweat trickling over his brow and onto his face. His mouth open wide.

And Brad heard Alden's silent scream, filled with

Learning Resources Center
Jordan High School
Jordan, Minnesota

a heart-breaking agony. The scream pierced the night, making Brad shudder.

"We hit something," Brad said aloud.

His voice sounded hollow and strange to him.

As if someone were standing nearby, standing and speaking for him. His hands clenched and slowly unclenched.

"We hit something that was alive," he whispered.

Alive.

And now dead.

I'm sure of it.

This is the spot.

The very spot.

And yet there is no sign of any accident.

I don't see any.

There must be.

It only happened last night.

Brad knelt in front of the car just as Alden had done. His face was pale in the cold glare of the headlights. He searched about the front wheels. Then on the sides.

There must be something left here, he said to himself. Bits of headlight glass. Some spots of dried blood. Shreds of ripped clothing. A button torn off a jacket.

He slowly straightened up and stood in the darkness thinking, his face grim and white.

There was nothing. It was as if someone had come and swept the road and its sides clean. Not a trace of anything.

Who could have done it? And why?

And the body? Where is it?

Was it the body of an animal? A dog?

A person?

Taken away. As if nothing happened here. Nothing.

But now I know it did happen.

It did.

Someone was killed.

Killed instantly without a sound or even a murmur. But killed. Killed.

Brad went back to his car, opened the glove compartment, and took out a flashlight.

He walked very slowly down the road, the beam splitting the darkness, his eyes searching. But the road was smooth and clean.

He turned and walked back to the car, this time along the narrow shoulder of the road.

Nothing. Clean.

All too clean, he thought grimly. Not even a cast-off cigarette butt.

He went off the road and into the field of grass. An old beer can. He picked it up and threw it bitterly far into the night.

As he turned to go back to the car, he saw a faint gleam on the ground ahead of him. He walked through the rustling grass to the gleam, his pulse quickening.

Brad stooped and picked up a small piece of rounded metal. Then he held it close to the flashlight's beam.

It was a pocket watch. A small gold pocket watch with a ribbon attached to it. It felt cold to his hand, cold and chilling.

He turned the watch over and read the initials engraved on its back.

P.M.H.

He was about to put the watch into his pocket when he noticed a stain on the ribbon. He held the ribbon up, close to the flashlight's beam. It could be mud, he thought. It could be. But then his heart began to pound within him.

Blood. It looks like dried blood, he said to himself. It looks very much like it.

His hand tightened about the watch and he stood tense in the night, his eyes upon the tree. The gnarled branches stretched fiercely into the dark sky. A thin ray of moonlight touched the branches. A ray of eerie moonlight.

Brad stood gazing at the tree, lost in a well of silence. Suddenly he heard a piercing scream just behind him. He shivered and swung about.

Then he saw the large glowing eyes of the cat. Like the large glowing eyes of a black panther. The cat screamed again. The sound cut through the silence like a ripping blade. And then the glowing eyes melted back into the vast darkness of the night.

All was still again.

Brad breathed out low and then slowly walked back to the car. He got in and started up the motor.

Then he swung the car around and turned down the road, back toward his house.

He drove slowly, his face grim with thought.

The watch in his pocket.

The stain of blood on its ribbon.

8

He sat in the kitchen watching the blue, wavering flame of the gas jet. After a while he got up and killed the flame. He poured coffee into a cup and went back to the table. He sat there drinking the coffee. He had been sitting there in the kitchen all the long hours since he had come back from Wilson Lane. Just sitting there. Brooding. Once he dozed off from sheer weariness. Only once.

Brad finished the coffee and then looked up at the kitchen clock. It was now nine in the morning.

He sighed and then went into the hallway and picked up the phone and dialed Alden's number.

Alden's father, Judge Peter Whitlock, answered.

"Is this Bradley?"

"Yes, Judge."

"How are your folks? Enjoying themselves?" The voice was quiet and measured.

Brad could see the tall, solid figure of the man as if before him. The rugged stern face. The brown studying eyes.

"They're fine," Brad said.

"Well, when you speak to them give my best regards."

"I will."

"How long will they be staying in Hawaii?"

"I really don't know. Maybe another week or two. They'll see as they go along. They're sort of playing it by ear."

He heard the Judge's soft chuckle. "Playing it by ear."

"Yes."

"That's the way to do it, Bradley. We must always make adjustments to life. That's the wise way to live."

"I guess it is," Brad said.

"You'll learn as you get older. We must compromise at times. Make adjustments to situations. That's the way to do it."

"Yes, Judge."

"You'll learn. You're young yet. You want to speak to Alden?"

"Yes."

"I'll put him on."

"Thanks, Judge."

But Peter Whitlock did not put down the phone. "Oh, Bradley," he said.

"Yes?"

"I understand you two drank a bit too much the other night."

The quiet, measured voice had become severe.

Brad was silent.

"You'd better tone it down, Bradley."

"I'm sorry, Judge."

"Being sorry is not enough. Sooner or later you'll do something that you'll regret. So tone it down, son. You and Alden."

"I will."

"Remember now. I'm a tolerant man. But don't abuse my tolerance. Neither you nor Alden."

Brad didn't speak.

"And if you're wondering how I found out about your excessive drinking that night, I have very reliable information that you were seen swimming in the Sound. And then the two of you ran up and down the beach stark naked. Singing and shouting loud enough to wake up the dead."

"Saw me?"

"Yes. The two of you."

"Are you sure of that, Judge?"

"Are you questioning me, Bradley? Of course, I'm sure." The voice had risen slightly in a controlled anger.

I wasn't in the water, Brad said to himself.

I never ran on that beach.

Never.

I know I didn't.

Know it in my very bones.

"I don't want you drinking and driving anymore, Bradley. Neither you nor Alden. Is that clear to you?"

"Yes," Brad said.

He heard the man's voice again and this time it was softer. "You're like another son to me, Bradley. You know that."

"Yes, Judge."

"I'll let you speak to Alden."

Brad waited in silence.

Then he heard Alden's bright voice. "Brad?"

"Yes, Alden."

"Up early, old buddy?"

"Right."

"Ready for the day? It's a great one coming up."

"Yes." And he thought to himself, is it a great day, Alden?

"You sound a little down, Brad."

"I'm okay."

"Down. The Judge give you one of his lectures?" The voice was bright and easy but Brad felt that there was something underneath it. Something he couldn't define. But it was there, like a dark, glinting thread.

"He did, Alden."

"I thought so."

There was the slightest of pauses and then Alden spoke again.

"Pay it no mind. There was a little storm here. But the weather's clearing up again."

"Okay, Alden," Brad said.

"Forget it. Sunshine for the rest of the day."

Alden then laughed. His pleasant easy laugh. It was always good to hear that laugh, Brad thought somberly. But not good now.

Brad waited and then spoke. "I want to talk to you, Alden."

"What about?"

"I'll tell you when I see you."

"Sure thing. Come on over."

"I will."

"I'm on the tennis court. Playing with Cathy."

Cathy was Alden's younger sister. She was tall, blond, and extremely good-looking, just like Alden. The two could have been twins. She liked Brad, very much. But he could never warm up to her.

"Cathy's giving me a hard game. That pro she's taking lessons with is going to make her a tournament player," Alden said.

44

And she will become one, Brad thought. A good one. Maybe that's why I can't get close to her. She drives too much. Underneath there's always a tension in her. And it makes me uneasy. She never seems to be at rest. Always trying to get there. And she'll walk over anybody who's in her way. And smile while she's doing it.

And yet I like her, he thought. In a strange, strange way. But I'll never be able to get close to her.

With Alden it's different. He just stands by and takes things easy. Like it's all coming to him. And it does come to him. He was born a champion. Yes, I guess that's it.

He heard himself speak to Alden. "I'd like to talk to you alone."

"Alone?"

"Yes, Alden."

"Something heavy come up?"

"Could be."

"What is it?"

"We'll talk and I'll tell you."

"Sure thing, Brad. Sure thing."

And Alden laughed. Brad listened to that smooth, warm laugh and for an instant it made him smile. But only for an instant.

"Bring your racket. Cathy wants to try to beat you. I told her no way, José. You're the best around."

"I'm not in the mood, Alden."

"Bring it. There's always time to talk. It's a long day. What do you say, old buddy?"

"Okay," Brad said quietly.

Then he put down the phone.

9

On the way to the tennis courts, Brad saw Alden's white Jaguar parked in the long, winding driveway, next to one of the closed garage doors. He went over to it slowly and stood gazing at it. The sleek car gleamed in the late morning sunlight. A sunlight cold and clean. He thought of the dark night and trembled.

His eyes searched the front of the car and then fastened onto the two glistening headlights. There was not a mark on either of them, nor anywhere else on the gleaming front of the car. Yet he remembered Alden kneeling on the road, the bits of headlight glass glittering in the palm of his big hand.

Brad knelt in front of the headlights.

One or both were shattered, he said to himself. It had to be. I saw those bits of glass. Saw them through my half-closed eyes. But I saw them.

Then he heard a voice.

"What is it, Brad?"

He turned sharply and saw a woman standing close to him. He paled and straightened up.

"Brad?" It was Alden's mother. There was an anxious, questioning look in her hazel eyes.

"Just admiring the car, Mrs. Whitlock," he said in a low voice.

"Is anything wrong?"

He shook his head silently.

"You've seen this car many times before," she said.

"I know."

"You've even driven it."

"Yes."

"Many times, Brad."

He didn't speak.

She reached out and put her hand on his.

Her voice when she spoke was soft and almost plaintive.

"Please tell me, Brad."

She was a small and still pretty woman who was always quiet and almost withdrawn. She listened most of the time and rarely spoke. Brad often felt that there was an aura of sadness about her. He didn't know why it was there. His mother had once said that it was because the Judge dominated her too much. He and the rest of the Whitlocks. Gave her no breathing space. But Brad felt it was something else.

"It's really nothing. Nothing," he murmured.

"You boys get into any trouble with the car?"

"No," he said quickly. "Not at all, Mrs. Whitlock."

"Are you sure, Brad?"

"Yes."

She just looked at him and, for a moment, Brad

thought that she was going to speak again, but she didn't. She turned silently away and walked toward the huge, sprawling white house. It was then that Brad saw the tall, solid figure of Judge Whitlock standing on the patio. Standing there gazing at Brad. With a cold, steely look in his eyes.

10

All the time he was on the court with Cathy he was thinking.

How well do I know the Whitlocks?

Brad looked over to where Alden was lounging in a chair, a towel around his neck, his long legs stretched out before him, his damp, blond hair glistening in the sun, an easy, careless look on his handsome face.

How well?

I've been with the Whitlocks all my life. Grew up with Alden.

How well?

They're a clan all their own. You never really get to know them. I can see that now. Now that I've asked that question for the first time in my life.

"Brad, you've just missed an easy shot."

"Did I, Cathy?"

"Yes. Stop horsing around with me."

"I'm not."

"You are."

"I couldn't reach the ball. You placed it perfectly."

"Stop it."

She came up to the net, her blue eyes hard on him, hard and commanding.

"I want your best game or none at all," she said. "Is that clear to you?"

You stand like a queen, he thought. A tall, blonde queen.

"It's clear to me, Cathy," he said.

"Your best."

He grinned at her. "You'll get it."

"Even if you wipe me out."

"Sure thing."

She turned abruptly away from him and took up her position on the court. She crouched, tense and waiting for his serve.

"Cathy's playing better all the time," Alden called out to him. "Took a set from me and almost got the other one."

"Alden, I'm trying to concentrate," Cathy said.

"Made her more arrogant than ever, if that's possible," Alden laughed.

"Shut up. You drink too much," she said.

"Now why did you say that?"

"Because you drink too much. You drink and drive. One day you're going to get into a real mess."

Brad saw a sudden dark expression come into Alden's eyes as he looked at his sister.

"You talk too much, Cathy."

Cathy turned back to Brad. "Let's get going."

How well do I know you, old buddy? Brad

thought as he served an ace. You Whitlocks know how to wear masks. To cover up. And he thought the words again. Cover up.

For some reason he could not comprehend, Brad felt a cold anger sweep through him. An anger at Cathy and Alden. At all the Whitlocks.

He reached back and served an ace and then another. Then he hit a ball that twisted away from Cathy's reach. She dropped the racket and looked over the net to him, a puzzled expression on her face.

Suddenly, he heard Alden's voice. "Wipe her out, Brad. Give her a good lesson. She's too arrogant."

Cathy didn't say anything.

Alden laughed, his easy, warm laugh, but the dark look was still deep in his eyes. "Make her feel like a loser," he said. "Do it, Brad."

How well do I know you? Brad thought. The anger was still with him. He smashed a return just out of Cathy's reach. She tried for it desperately and then stumbled and fell.

"That's it, Brad." He heard Alden's cruel laugh and he saw tears come to Cathy's eyes. She looked so forlorn and defeated.

Brad felt a pang of remorse sweep over him. He took it easy with her after that. When the set was over she walked away without a word.

Alden lounged in his chair, his bronze face now calm and impassive, like a mask.

11

"You wanted to talk, old buddy," Alden said.

"Yes."

They were sitting alone on the tennis court, side by side.

"Something heavy?"

"Yes, Alden."

"What about?"

Brad hesitated and didn't speak.

"Well?" Alden said.

"Let's take a ride, Alden."

Alden looked calmly at Brad. "Where to?"

"Along the Beach Highway."

"Why there?"

Brad shrugged and didn't answer. He stared silently at the long shadows that fell over one end of the court. Then he spoke.

"Just feel like looking out over the water."

Alden smiled but his eyes were studying Brad's profile. "Want to go sailing?" he asked.

"No."

"My boat? Marian's? I'll call her up," Alden said.

Brad shook his head.

"Something's bugging you, old buddy."

"Something is," Brad murmured.

A gray squirrel ran along the shadows and then suddenly flashed into the sunlight, showering sparks of light. And then it was gone. Only the shadows remained, dark and foreboding. Brad kept staring at them.

Alden stood up. "Okay," he said. "Let's take the ride."

Brad looked up at him.

"In your car, Alden. The Jag."

Nothing showed on Alden's face.

I feel that you know what's in me, Brad thought. What's weighing so heavily on my heart. I feel you do.

And yet . . . ?

Brad slowly got up and followed Alden to his car.

12

The sun was sparkling off the water and, as they drove
down the highway, Alden began to sing in a loud,
clear voice.

"My name is Yon Yonson
I come from Wisconsin
I work in the lumber yard there
I walk down the street
And the people I meet
They ask me
What is your name?
And I tell them
My name is Yon Yonson
I come from—"
"Alden," Brad said.
Alden stopped singing and turned to him. "Yes?"
"The other night."
"What other night?"

"The night of the party," Brad said.

"Oh."

"Where did you go in swimming? Do you remember?"

"Sure."

"Let's stop there for a minute," Brad said.

"Sure thing."

Brad thought he saw Alden's face pale just a bit. But he wasn't sure.

"Alden."

"Yes?"

"You say I went in swimming with you?"

"That's right."

They drove silently along the highway and then Alden began singing again.

"My name is Yon Yonson ..."

Brad thought his voice was just a bit lower, and not as carefree.

"I come from Wisconsin
I work in the lumber yard there
And the people I meet
They ask me—"

Alden suddenly stopped singing and pulled the car onto the shoulder of the road. He smiled at Brad. "It was here," he said, pointing to a toppled lifeguard stand and then out to the reach of blue sparkling water. "That's where you went in with me."

Far out, close to the horizon was the black gleam of a small freighter. The beach was white and empty.

Brad gazed at the slow-moving boat, the wisp of black smoke trailing lazily up into the blue sparkling sky. He finally spoke.

"I never went in with you, Alden."

Alden was silent.

"And I never ran on the beach with you."

"Marian and Eliot saw you."

"I never did it," Brad said.

Alden slowly turned to him, his blue eyes clear and penetrating. "What's the point, old buddy?" he said.

"The point is that I remember some things pretty clearly."

"Some things?"

"That's right," Brad said.

"For instance?"

"I saw something happen, Alden."

"You did?"

"Yes."

"What was it?" Alden said.

Brad looked away from the penetrating eyes and didn't answer. He kept staring out to the distant, shimmering horizon until he found again the slow-moving freighter.

A great sadness enveloped him as he watched the small black shape, the trailing spiral of smoke being lost in a vast sparkling sky. Lost. Forever lost.

We're moving away from each other, Alden, he said to himself. And we are such good friends. I thought we would be friends to the end of our lives. Like the sun in the sky. Like that.

He heard Alden's voice, patient and calm. "Well, Brad?"

Brad slowly turned back to him. "Let's go down Wilson Lane and I'll tell you."

He saw Alden's hand tighten over the steering wheel. "Why Wilson Lane?"

"Just let's do it."

Alden's hand relaxed its grip. "Okay, Brad. You're calling the shots today."

"I guess I am," Brad said.

56

Alden swung the car off the shoulder and back onto the highway. He turned slightly and smiled his easy smile at Brad. "You've been having some bad dreams, old buddy," he said. "Some real bad dreams." Then he laughed and began to sing Yon Yonson.

This time his voice was loud and carefree again.

13

They drove down Wilson Lane past the scattered wooden houses that even in the sparkling sunshine looked gray and forlorn, their shadeless windows empty and coldly glittering.

Alden stopped singing and now the two friends were silent. Sitting side by side.

Then the tree came softly into sight and Brad spoke. "Slow down, Alden."

"Sure thing."

Brad watched as they came closer and closer to the tree, the gnarled tree with its bare branches reaching hopelessly into the blazing, uncaring sky. Its twisted branches. Like severed arms.

"Stop the car, Alden," he said in a hollow voice. "By the tree."

The car stopped.

Then the vast silence rushed in and enveloped them.

As Brad sat there gazing at the wide, empty fields of tall grass, the bitter, the terrifying night came back to him. Vivid and strong.

He saw again, through half-shut eyes, Alden kneeling in front of the car. The headlights shining into his pale face. The mouth dropping open with a silent, agonized cry.

Then the night just past blended in and he heard again the piercing scream of the cat just behind him. He shivered. And stared into the yellow, glowing eyes.

"No," he whispered.

He felt Alden's strong hand on his shoulder.

He heard his voice.

"What's wrong, old buddy?" Alden said.

Brad turned, pale and shaken, and looked into Alden's calm and composed face.

"Alden," he said in a tight voice.

"Yes?"

"The other night, you stopped the car right by this tree."

"I don't follow you, Brad."

"You stopped and then got out of the car and—"

"I never went down Wilson Lane," Alden cut in softly. Ever so softly.

"You did."

Alden smiled compassionately. "I said you've been having bad dreams, old buddy."

"Don't give me that."

"Brad, you were drunk. Out like a light."

"No."

"You don't even remember swimming or running on the beach."

"Cut it out, Alden."

"I'm just giving you the truth, Brad."

Brad pointed desperately to the tree. "You stopped the car here," he said.

Alden shook his head. His voice was calm and level. "We never went down this road."

"You did," Brad said.

And he wanted to shout, Take off the mask, Alden. Take it off. Face the truth. Face it.

But Alden just sat there. One hand lay carelessly upon the wheel. The sun glinted off his blond hair.

Brad got out of the car and slammed the door shut. The sound ripped through the silence like a gunshot.

"You were here, Alden. Here."

He knelt in front of the headlights and looked up to where Alden still sat in the car, quiet and composed. Yet Brad could see that Alden's eyes had become dark and penetrating.

"Alden, I saw you kneel like this. And there were bits of headlight glass in your hand. In your hand, Alden."

"Never happened, Brad. Never."

"You hit something. You did."

"Do you see any sign on the car? Any?"

"No."

"I hit nothing."

"You could have had the car repaired."

"I could have. But I didn't. Because there was no need to."

Brad was silent.

"Get back in the car and let's get out of here," Alden said quietly.

Brad didn't move.

Alden smiled. "You're starting to get under my skin, old buddy."

Brad shook his head fiercely. "No. You come out here."

"Why?"

"I want you standing beside me. Right where I am."

"Brad."

"Do it, Alden."

"You're out of your skull."

"Do it," Brad said.

"I'm telling you for the last time we were never down this road."

"We were."

Alden looked silently at him, just a hint of a smile in the calm blue eyes.

"You hit something, Alden. I heard a thud. I know I did."

"Drunk as you were," Alden murmured.

"Drunk as I was."

"You were out cold. Asleep."

"I saw your face. I heard you scream," Brad said.

Alden's lips suddenly tightened. His voice was low and hard when he spoke. "Are you going to stop this?"

Brad grimly shook his head. "What did you hit, Alden?"

Alden didn't answer.

"Tell me."

Alden abruptly switched on the motor. "I'm going."

"What happened, Alden? Who was it?"

"Get out of my way."

But Brad still stood there. "Was it a man? What happened to him?"

"Brad," Alden shouted. "Look out." His foot hit the accelerator hard and the car jumped forward and Brad moved to the side just in time. The car swept by him.

He slowly turned and watched the Jaguar disappear down the winding road, the blond head of the driver sparkling in the sun, finally becoming a tiny blot. Then, it too was gone. The silence rushed in. Cold and chilling. He was now alone.

"Alden," he murmured.

The shadows of the tree's bare branches fell across him. Like black, iron bars. He felt their weight across his chest. Within him he heard again the savage scream of the cat.

"Someone died here," he whispered.

"Someone died."

14

Brad was walking along the lonely, winding road when he heard the dim sound of a car coming up from behind him. He thought it might be Alden coming back to pick him up, but he knew it was a hopeless thought, that the past was swiftly and inevitably breaking up, never to be put together again.

As the car neared him he saw that it was an old Chevrolet with out-of-state license plates. Illinois. Chicago.

A bumper sticker: Save the Environment. Another sticker: House the Homeless. On the dusty hood, a small insignia of the Chicago Bears football team.

The dark blue car pulled up close to him and stopped.

"Are you from around here?" It was a girl's voice.

He turned and looked at her. "Yes."

She was alone in the car.

"Am I on Wilson Lane?" she asked.

He nodded.

"I'm trying to find eight Wilson Lane."

She was about his age, with clear, pleasant features. Not pretty and not plain, he thought idly.

"The houses don't seem to have any numbers," he said. "They're empty and nobody really lives in them."

"I got a letter from number eight," she said.

He shrugged and didn't say anything. He waited for her to drive off and leave him alone. He was still thinking of the night. The night that was coming down like a wall between him and Alden. A dark, impenetrable wall.

"You walking?"

She wore a checkered shirt and jeans.

He didn't answer.

"Want a lift while you help me find the house?" she said.

Her hair was long and honey-colored. Her face looked tired and drawn. But her gray eyes were smiling. A pleasant smile. Not pretty and not plain, he thought. But the kind that could grow on you. That's the dangerous kind. You get caught up with them and they never let go.

He heard her soft, tired voice. "I've come all the way from Chicago. Almost nonstop. I'm beat."

Yes. You are, he thought.

He got into the car and sat down next to her.

"You find number eight for me and then I'll take you to where you're going. How's that for a deal?"

"Okay," he said.

"As long as it's not in the next state."

He smiled. "It's not too far from here."

"Good enough."

They drove along without speaking until one of the desolate, gray houses came into sight.

"I'll try this one," he said.

She pulled the car over to the side of the road and he got out and walked through the gently swishing grass until he came to the weather-beaten front of the old house. There was no number to be seen.

He knocked on the paint-peeled door but no one came to answer. Then he turned the old brass knob, opened the creaking door, and went inside. He stood in the shadowy corridor and called out, listening to his loud, piercing voice echo throughout the empty, ghostly house. Then he waited.

There was no sound of an answering human voice.

Brad heard the rapid scurrying of rats' feet on the wooden floor above him and then there was cold, eerie silence.

A sense of rage and desolation came over him.

He remembered having a lazy but serious discussion with Alden, late at night, a summer night. They were sitting out alone on the empty, bare tennis court and Alden was saying: "When it's all over, Brad, after the big blast, we noble and sacred human beings will be swept off this charred earth like dead flies and the rats will take over. Swarms and swarms of them." A soft, sad light had come into Alden's eyes: "Maybe it will be a good thing. Because we're nothing but a bunch of killers. We kill minds, we kill hearts, and we kill bodies. And then we put on our brightly painted masks and smile and bow to each other. As if we're dancers in a delicate and intricate ballet. What do you say, old buddy? Huh? What do you say?" Then he put his arm around Brad and laughed his easy, melodic laugh.

Brad turned and went out of the house, closing the door behind him.

He stood there, looking over the stretch of grass to where the girl sat in the car, an expectant, hopeful look on her tired face.

Brad shook his head. He came back to the car and got in. "Nobody's in there. No number," he said.

She looked away from him and out over the fields. A soft wind came up and rippled the grass.

"Let's try another one," he said gently. Somehow he felt sorry for her.

"Okay," she sighed.

"I'm Brad."

"Ellen."

"You live in Chicago?"

She nodded. "With my aunt. We have a big old house. Just the two of us."

"Sounds like a good arrangement," Brad said.

"It is. We like each other."

"That always means a lot."

"It does," Ellen said.

He glanced at her profile as she drove. Not pretty and not plain, he thought. No. More pretty than plain.

"You go to school there?" he asked.

"One of the small colleges. First year."

"Finished or going into?"

"Finished. I should have said second year."

She's about a year older than I, he thought.

He heard her speak. "You? How about you?"

"I'll be going to college out here. In September," Brad said.

"What are you heading for?"

"You mean what career?" he asked.

She nodded.

"I don't know yet. How about you?"

She swung away from a deep rut in the road and then spoke. "My aunt's a school principal. Many years. She wants me to go into teaching. Feels she can help me along."

"And?"

"I'm for social work," Ellen said.

"Why that?"

"Why?"

"Uh-huh."

She suddenly turned to him.

"People," she said. "I'm interested in people. And what happens to them. Especially poor people. They're not getting a fair shake. Never have."

A soft, earnest light had come into the tired gray eyes. You have pretty eyes, he thought. They didn't look that pretty when I first got into the car.

"I come off a Nebraska farm, Brad. My father had it taken away from him. Do you think that's fair? Our home? He worked his heart out on that farm. Well? Tell me."

Brad didn't speak.

"He mortgaged his farm to buy more equipment. He listened to the government agents. They told him to increase his yield. They were going to sell millions of tons of wheat overseas. Then the whole thing fell apart. And he was stuck. He and many other farmers. The banks came in and took away the farms. It wasn't his fault. It wasn't the other farmers' fault. Stuck and thrown off their lands. Is that fair? Is it?"

"I haven't really thought much about that," he said.

"Because you don't know," Ellen said.

"I don't know."

She stared at him. "And the homeless? You don't think about them?"

"I never see them," Brad said.

"So they don't exist for you."

He smiled wanly at her. "In a way they don't."

"But they're all over. In the cities. Living on the streets. Wandering the highways. And they don't exist for you?"

He was silent.

"You don't think about them?" Ellen said.

"No."

"Then you should. You should."

"I guess I should," he said.

She looked down the road for a while without speaking.

"My father's one of them. Homeless," she said in a low voice. "He's been wandering around the country. I'm trying to catch up with him now." She turned to him. "How are your folks? You live with them?"

"Yes."

"Get along with them?"

"Uh-huh. They're pretty easy to get along with," Brad said.

"Kind of let you do what you want."

"That's it. And yet . . ."

"And yet what?"

He didn't speak.

"And yet you'd like to be closer?" Ellen said.

He shrugged. "They're in Hawaii now on vacation. They wanted me to go along. But I didn't. Just wanted to be here with my friends."

"That's natural."

He looked at her. "Yes. I guess it is," he said.

"What does your father do?" Ellen asked.

"He's an executive in a large law firm."

"President?"

"Vice president."

"You look like the son of a president," she smiled.

He laughed.

"And your mother, Brad?"

"She runs a real estate agency. Owns it."

"Then you live well. High off the hog," Ellen said.

"We live well."

"Have your own car?"

"Yes."

"What make?"

"A Ford Taurus."

"Let me guess. It's a '90."

"Late '89," Brad said.

"You get a good allowance?"

"Pretty good one."

"Ever work?" Ellen asked.

He shook his head.

"Out my way, you don't work you don't eat," she said. "But that's out my way. The world's a strange place, isn't it, Brad?"

He didn't say anything.

"I've always worked," she said. "On the farm and then after the farm was lost. I still work and go to school."

"What do you do?"

"I'm a waitress in a Yuppie restaurant. The tips are good and the fellows are fresh. Makes life interesting."

"And the women Yuppies?"

"They're snippy and unbearable. But they're all right."

She laughed and then they went silent.

After a while she spoke again.

"High off the hog. And so you never think of the homeless and the poor. Why should you?"

She tapped him gently on the shoulder and her

tired gray eyes looked fully into his for an instant. He felt a quivering inside him, pleasant and warm.

"You're a spoiled brat, Brad," she said softly.

He grinned.

"I guess I am."

Her eyes were still on him. She does grow on you, he thought. Grows fast.

He heard her soft, almost taunting voice. "And with your good looks and sensitive brown eyes I'll bet the girls around here spoil you rotten. Isn't that so?" she said.

He didn't answer.

She smiled and turned to the road again. "People, Brad," she murmured. "People. Get with it."

And it was then that a house came into view.

"We'll try this one," he said.

"Okay."

"Maybe we'll be lucky this time, Ellen," he said.

He found it easy to say her name. As if he had been saying it for a long time.

She drove on and then pulled the car over to the side of the road and he got out. And as he did, something within him told him that this was the house. He walked up the grassy path to the front door. He knocked a few times, knocked hard, and then the door slowly swung open.

15

An old, white-haired man with a lined, weather-beaten face stood looking down at him. He was lean and very tall.

"Yes?" The voice was soft and pleasant.

"Sorry to trouble you," Brad said.

"No trouble."

"Is this number eight?"

"Used to be. It's nothing now. Just plain nothing," the old man said. He wore old, faded overalls and torn sneakers.

"But it's number eight?"

"Well, if you want to call it that."

"Anybody live here with you?" Brad asked.

"Why?" The pale blue eyes that had been friendly now became wary.

"My friend is trying to find her father. She's come all the way from Chicago."

"Chicago? That's a long ways from here."

"It is," Brad said.

The man's eyes had become friendly again.

"Lived there years ago. Years and years ago. Before you were born. Her father?"

Brad nodded. "She got a letter from him. Came from this number."

"I see."

"Anybody here with you?"

"Just a few drifters," the man said. "They're out looking for day work. They come and go. I stay on. Nowhere else to go to. Too old to move on anymore."

"Mind if I call her over?" Brad asked.

"No. Got a few cents eating money you could spare?"

"Sure." Brad took a dollar out of his wallet and handed it to the old man.

"Thanks, son. I used to work in the stockyards in Chicago. A slugger. Hard work it was. Real hard work. Wore me out. I never was the same after that. Took my years away."

The old man smiled a sad smile and tucked the dollar away deep in his pocket and as he did, the leg of the overalls hitched up and Brad saw that the man had no socks on. It made him suddenly think of Alden walking the deck of Marian's sailboat wearing white sneakers but no socks. He didn't know why he thought of that.

"Worked the stockyards," the old man said. "And when they closed up I went over to Omaha. Worked the stockyards there. And then my wife up and left me and I started wandering around. The years wandering with me. And now I'm here." He sighed softly. "Call her in," he said.

Brad turned to the doorway and waved to Ellen

to come out of the car. He watched her hurry over to him, an eager look on her face. You're taller than I thought, he said to himself. And you walk with such easy grace. Even in those old jeans. No wonder the Yuppies get fresh with you.

"This is the house, Ellen," he said. "But he's alone now. The others are out."

She turned to the old man. "They'll be back?" she asked.

"They should. What does your daddy look like?"

"He's a stocky man with brown hair turning gray. He has a scar on his right cheek. A long scar. And he has—"

"Sounds familiar to me," the man cut in. "What's his name?"

"Paul."

"Paul what?"

"Paul Hanson."

"Yes," the old man said. "I know him."

"And?"

"He was here."

"Was?" Ellen asked and her voice shook.

"Well, he went out the other night for a walk to the beach and he never came back. So I guess he moved on."

"He couldn't have."

The old man shook his head. "That's how it is with them," he said. "They suddenly take off and are gone. They travel light. Very light. Leave nothing behind."

Ellen looked away from him to Brad. "He wrote me he would stay and wait for me. He wanted to talk to me. To see if I could get him back with my aunt. He was tired of the road. He wanted to come back and live with us in the big house and put his life together.

73

If she would let him. She never forgave him for walking out on my mother."

Her voice choked up and then she went on. "It was as if he was begging for his life back."

Brad didn't speak.

"He never came back," the old man said finally.

"I hadn't heard from him in three years. And then I got this letter," Ellen said.

"Just never came back. I'm sorry."

"And he left nothing here?"

"Nothing. Had nothing but his clothes on when he came here."

"Maybe he will come back."

"Maybe. But I don't see it likely."

Ellen suddenly turned away from them and walked slowly back to the car. Her shoulders sagged.

Brad could see how tired and defeated she was.

"Looks like she's crying," the old man said. "No tears showing on that young girl's face but she's crying."

"Yes," Brad murmured.

"Go after her and comfort her," the man said gently. "She's your girlfriend, isn't she?"

Brad nodded.

When he caught up to Ellen there were no tears showing in her eyes. But her face was pale and slack.

"Came all this way to miss him," she said wearily.

"What are you going to do now?" he asked.

"I don't know."

He was silent.

"All this way. From Chicago to Connecticut. That's a long, long way to drive. Mile after mile after mile. The night never seemed to end. And I miss him."

"Maybe it wasn't meant to be," he said in a low voice.

"Maybe it wasn't."

But then he saw her face tighten up and her eyes become hard.

"No," she said. "I'm staying around. He'll come back. I know he will."

Brad turned away from her and gazed out at the sunswept horizon.

"He'll show up," she said quietly.

He slowly turned back to her.

"Where are you going to stay, Ellen?" he asked.

"Oh. I'll camp out somewhere."

He stared at her. "What?"

"I'm a waitress, Brad. My money's limited. I can't afford a motel. Especially around here."

"But camp out?"

Ellen nodded. "I've done it before. There's a beach here, isn't there?"

"A few miles down."

"Which way?"

He pointed.

"A large one?" she asked.

"Yes."

"Large enough so I can find a spot all my own? Away from people?"

"It's pretty empty most of the time," Brad said.

"Any diners nearby?"

"Yes. On the highway."

"And the highway runs along the beach."

"It does."

"I'll hit the beach," Ellen said.

He didn't speak.

"You look shocked," she smiled. Then she turned and got into the car.

He still stood there.

"Come on, Brad. I'll drive you home."

"Home?"

"Where you live."

"Oh."

"That was our deal, wasn't it?"

"Yes," he said slowly. "That was our deal." He got into the car.

When he looked at her face as she drove along the bleak and lonely road, he saw that it was sad and drawn.

16

Ellen pulled into the driveway and stopped the car.

"You live in a very nice house," she said.

Brad didn't say anything. He had spoken little during the entire ride. Just sat there, looking ahead of him, down the winding, dusty road. Once he gave her directions and then he was silent again. Thinking. Ever thinking. Of the night. The dark, dark night. The night that had come silently from out of nowhere, come silently, steadily, and inexorably into his life. Never to leave him. Never.

He heard her voice. "You have a pool?"

"Yes."

"I'll bet everybody has a pool around here," Ellen said.

"About everybody."

She glanced away from him to the house again. "It's lovely. You do live high off the hog, Brad."

"Ellen," he said.

She turned back to him. "Yes?"

He looked directly at her. "I'm going to ask you something."

"Go ahead."

He hesitated an instant and then spoke. "What kind of a man was your father?"

"Why?"

"Just interested."

"Why?"

"Because you interest me."

She smiled and then spoke. "He wasn't good to me or my mother. If that's what you're after."

"Go on," Brad said.

"Just walked out when the farm was taken away and he never came back. Do you think your father would do that to your mother if he lost everything?"

Brad shook his head. "No. They love each other too much."

They were silent and then she spoke in a soft voice and there was a hint of sadness in it. "Maybe I'm too hard on him for that. He was a broken man. But just the same, he should've stayed on. We got ourselves two rooms in town. We needed him around." She looked away from him and was silent.

"And your mother?" he asked.

"She didn't last long. She died."

"Because he walked out?"

"That and other things," Ellen said. "Why do I tell you this? And why do you want to know it?"

He shrugged silently.

"Let's leave it alone, Brad. Okay?"

"Sure," he said.

She looked at him again and then touched his shoulder gently. "Time for me to go."

"I guess so," he murmured.

"Thanks for helping me out. It was very nice of you."

"Was really nothing."

He slowly got out of the car and then stood there looking at her.

She waited.

"Ellen," he said.

"Yes?"

"You say you're going to be around for a few days?"

"I intend to."

"And you're going to camp out on the beach?"

"Right."

She was smiling at him.

He stood there silent.

She broke the silence. "You mean you want to see me again?"

"That and something else," he said.

"What is it?"

He hesitated and then spoke. "Look, Ellen. I've got a big house here. Lots of room."

"So?"

"My folks are away. They won't be back for a while."

"And?"

"Just pick a room. Any one you want and ... and ...." His voice trailed away into silence.

She looked at him with her gray eyes and laughed softly. "You're starting to remind me of my Yuppies."

"But, Ellen."

She shook her head.

"Thanks. But no deal, Brad."

"Why not? It'll be like living in a hotel. You can come and go as you please. Nobody will bother you."

"Just let it alone."

"But why rough it out on the beach? It doesn't make sense."

"It makes sense."

"It can be dangerous out there. Especially at night."

"I can handle it," she said quietly.

He stood there silent and frustrated.

"You want to see me tomorrow?" she asked gently. Her voice was soft and warm. Her gray eyes were looking into his.

God, how pretty you've become, he said to himself. In such a short time.

"Well, Brad?"

"Sure," he said.

"What time do you want me to pick you up?"

"Any time you want."

"How about twelve? We'll have lunch together somewhere."

"Good enough."

"You'll pick the place," she said.

"Okay."

"Not too expensive. We'll Dutch it," she said.

"Why?"

"Because that's how I want it."

"But I have enough money. More than enough," Brad said.

"That's your money. Not mine."

A thin ray of sunshine fell between them, tinting her hair golden, softening her eyes.

"Ellen," he said.

"Yes?"

"I'm really glad I met you."

"Are you?"

"Yes."

"I am, too."

Then he watched her drive off. When he could see her no more, he turned and went into the house. A surge of joy in his heart.

17

He stood in the bedroom by the bureau and in his hand was the glistening gold watch. His face was pale. His eyes stared into the shadows.

P.M.H.

Could it be Paul Hanson? Could it?

What would she say to me if I told her I sat in a car that killed her father? What? A stricken look came into his eyes and his lips quivered. His hands clenched tight.

No. They're somebody else's initials. It has to be.

Why did she come into my life? Why? He set his teeth together to keep from crying out.

Why did I go to that party with Alden? Why did I get drunk? Why did I let him drive the car? Why? Why?

"Why?" he whispered.

Brad dropped the watch back into the drawer and turned and went out of the room.

18

As he walked down the steps to the kitchen, Brad said to himself, But do I know that anybody was killed? How? What proof do I really have? It's all speculation. Miserable speculation.

I found a watch. A ribbon. What else do I have? Nothing, fool. Nothing.

There's not a sign on the car. Not a trace on the road. Nothing, fool. Nothing.

No wonder Alden got angry with me. Why shouldn't he be? You have nothing, fool. Nothing.

Brad turned on the gas jet under the coffeepot and watched the blue, wavering flame.

Suddenly the night came rushing back. The black, black night. And he saw again the glowing eyes of the cat. And he heard again the piercing scream.

He trembled violently.

The yellow, glowing eyes of the cat would not

merge back into the night. They kept staring at him. Two sharp points of light. Stabbing into his soul.

I'm caught, he said to himself. Caught in something I can't handle. And I don't know where to turn.

I don't.

19

He was sitting on the back patio just as night was coming on when he heard Cathy's voice.

"Brad?"

He turned and saw her come out of the shadows toward him. Tall and lithe and blond. Easy and self-assured.

Camelot.

He thought of Alden.

Camelot.

The Judge.

Camelot.

You all live in Camelot, he thought to himself bitterly. High on a hill. A sunlit hill. Alone in Camelot. Far, far from the real world.

And he thought of Ellen's words, "Where I come from, if you don't work you don't eat."

"I brought your car back," Cathy said as she sat

down on a chair by him. "Alden's out on the driveway with the Jag. He'll take me back."

Brad didn't speak.

Over them, the leaves of a slim elm tree rustled in a passing breeze.

"What's going on between the two of you?" she said.

"Nothing, Cathy. Nothing."

She shook her head and looked at him. "He's angry at you. And you're angry at him."

"That happens with friends," he said in a low voice.

"Never happened before that I know."

"It did, Cathy. And it will again."

She turned her head and looked fully at him. "You're Alden's best friend. You always were."

"And he's mine."

"What is it? Please, Brad."

He didn't speak. The leaves in the elm tree rustled again. Softly. Almost a ghostly sound.

He heard her gentle voice weave through it.

"Does it have something to do with Marian?" she asked.

"Marian?"

"She likes you a lot."

"So?"

"I've seen the way she looks at you at times," Cathy said.

"And?"

"Did she make a pass at you?"

"What?"

"And did Alden find out?"

"Cathy," he said.

"Ridiculous?"

"What do you think?" Brad said.

She was silent.

"Cathy," he said.

"Yes?"

"You don't like Marian. But she's going to be in your life for a long time."

"Because the Judge wants her to be?" Cathy said.

He nodded. "Yes. And her folks want her to be a Whitlock. And beneath it all, Marian wants the same thing. The prestige and political power that your family has. The long and honored tradition. She wants to walk into the governor's mansion at the side of a Whitlock. With Alden. It's all that Marian really wants."

"And Alden?" Cathy said.

"What about Alden?"

"He doesn't care for her that much," she said. "I know that he doesn't. He pretends."

He puts on his mask, Brad thought. He dances the ballet.

Then he heard himself say to her. "Alden will do what the Judge wants. He always does."

"I'll never like her," Cathy said.

"Try to."

"Then what is it?" Cathy asked.

"What is what?"

"Between you and Alden?"

"I told you. Nothing important."

"It bothers me a lot."

"Don't let it," he said.

"I just can't help myself."

"You can, Cathy. Forget it."

He patted her arm.

She suddenly leaned over and kissed him softly on the cheek. Strangely, he felt that it was Ellen kissing him.

He quivered within. A warm, pleasant feeling went through him. He sensed Ellen standing close to him. Very close. Talking softly.

But it was Cathy's voice he heard.

"Everybody likes you, Brad," she said. "All my friends."

"Cut it out," he said gently.

"They do."

She got up. Tall and lithe and blond. And he thought again of Camelot.

"Thanks for being so nice to me on the tennis court this morning. I didn't deserve it," she said.

At the beginning I wasn't nice at all, he thought.

"Try and make up with Alden. Please, Brad."

"Sure."

Then she turned and walked back into the shadows. He was alone again.

20

At ten o'clock that night the phone rang. Brad thought it could be his folks calling. Just to say hello and to see how things were.

But then he picked up the phone and heard the voice, bright and easy and warm, as though nothing had happened between them. . . . "Hello, old buddy."

"Hello, Alden."

"What've you been doing?"

"Just sitting around."

"Same here. I went sailing with Marian this afternoon. She asked for you."

"Did she?"

"Shame you weren't along."

"Yes."

There was a slight pause. "Feel like playing some tennis?" Alden asked.

"Now?"

"Why not now?"

"I don't know. It's late."

"I'll put the lights on. Come on over."

Brad didn't say anything.

"Come on over. We'll play a set and then talk."

"Talk?"

"Sure," Alden said. "It's a beautiful night. Cool and breezy. We can have a great game. If you spot me a little handicap."

"All right."

"We'll talk and work things out, old buddy. Okay?"

"We'll talk," Brad said.

"Sure thing."

Then he heard Alden put down the phone.

21

Just as Brad was about to lock the front door and go out of the house, the phone rang again. He stood there hesitant, looking at his car, and then went in and picked up the receiver.

It was his father.

"Brad?"

"Hello, Dad."

"Good to hear your voice. Tried to get you the other night. You were out."

"I guess I was."

"Two nights ago. Tried a few times."

"I was at a party," Brad said.

"With Alden?"

"Yes."

"Have a good time?"

Brad didn't answer.

"Did you?"

"Yes," Brad said.

"Good to hear your voice."

"The same, Dad."

"How are things going?"

"Fine."

"Just fine? Or fine?" And his father laughed.

Brad smiled. "They're okay," he said.

"Okay? Or just okay?"

"Okay."

Both of them laughed.

"Shame you didn't want to come with us," his father said. "We're having a great time. I'm calling you from Kaui. We left the big island yesterday."

And Brad said to himself, If only I had gone with them. Why didn't I? Why? I wouldn't have been at that party with Alden. I wouldn't have sat in his car. Both of us drunk.

I would've been in Hawaii. In another world. On another planet. Away.

Why didn't I go with them? It's all so absurd. So meaningless. Just a little thing like not going with them and life becomes a hell. A little, little thing.

He heard his father's voice. "You can still come out if you want, Brad."

"How much longer are you going to stay?"

"A week or two. But if you come out we'll make it longer. We'll show you a great time, Brad."

He stood there hesitant.

"Well, son?"

His father rarely called him "Son."

And in that word, now expressed, Brad felt the inner yearning and love that the man almost never showed him. He really wants me there, Brad thought.

"Brad?"

"I think I'll stay around here," Brad said.

"Whatever you say."

Brad was silent.

"You need any money?"

"No, Dad."

And he wanted to say, I need something more than money. I need you. And I don't know how to tell you that.

There's a gap between us. It's been there for years. I don't know how it started. I don't know when it started. But it's there. It's there. And I don't know how to get over it to reach you. I don't.

"Here's your mother. Take care of yourself, Brad."

He sensed the disappointment in his father's voice. So expertly covered.

"I will, Dad."

Then he spoke to his mother. It was all warm and pleasant. It made him feel good speaking to her. She asked him to come out there. And he sensed his father standing at her side when she did so.

She asked him again, later on. And then her voice was gone. And he was alone in the house again.

Then he went out and locked the front door.

He stood for a long moment looking up at the dark and silent house.

And he asked himself, Is this large, elaborate house, with its broad, manicured front lawns, any different from the lonely, desolate houses on Wilson Lane? Some of their dusty windows broken and their long, yellowing grass uncut? People, homeless and lost, wandering in and out of them, without ever getting to really know each other, to care, to love one another?

Is my house any different?

Do I really know my father and mother?

Do they really know me?

He got into his car and drove off into the night.

22

Alden wiped his sweaty face and forehead with a white towel, with slow, even strokes, and then he draped the towel about his neck and shoulders and walked over to the light switch. A slow, easy walk. He paused at the switch and turned to Brad.

"That was a great game, Brad. You're playing better than ever."

"You ought to work on your backhand, Alden. That's your weakness."

"You attack it all the time."

"That's right," Brad said. "I go from my strength to your weakness. That's the game."

"Maybe I should really work on it."

"Try a few lessons with Cathy's pro."

Alden nodded, his blond hair glinting in the court lights. "That's a good suggestion. Maybe I'll do it."

"Just to set you straight. A few lessons will do it," Brad said.

"Good idea."

Alden turned out the lights and the moonlight came down, sweeping over the court and the surrounding trees. A vast stillness settled over everything. Alden looked about him thoughtfully and then walked slowly over to one of the court chairs and sat down.

Brad followed him.

Alden pointed to a chair near him. "Rest yourself," he said.

"Okay."

The two friends sat quietly looking out over the court and at the stand of larch and elm trees that gleamed silver in the broad and peaceful night.

Strange, Brad thought. I got into the excitement of the game and forgot everything. As if I had entered into another world. A world that has its own reality. I wonder if the same thing happened to Alden.

He glanced at his friend's profile. It was quiet and impassive.

You never know with Alden, he thought. You never know what goes on inside of him. Deep down.

Maybe he could say the same thing about me. Probably could. Who knows?

"Brad."

Brad didn't hear Alden's voice. He stared ahead of him to the stand of trees.

"Brad."

He thought he could see a figure standing close to one of the tall elms. But he wasn't sure.

"Yes, Alden?"

"I'm sorry I left you out on that road. Alone."

Brad didn't speak. The figure looked tall and solid. The Judge? Or am I imagining it? It doesn't move. A night shadow?

He heard Alden's low voice.

"You got under my skin. I almost rode you down."

"You almost did," Brad said.

"Could've hurt you bad."

"You could have, Alden."

"But I guess I knew you'd jump out of the way in time. You're a fine athlete. Great reflexes." He paused and then spoke again. "But I shouldn't have done it, Brad."

Brad didn't say anything.

"I lost control. Just lost it," Alden said.

And he was silent again.

Alden wiped his face with the towel and then threw the towel away from him onto the ground.

And as he did, he spoke. "You got under my skin. But you were right. You were right all along."

"What do you mean?" Brad said.

The towel lay on the ground, crumpled and white. A ragged gleam in the darkness.

"I didn't tell you the truth, old buddy." Alden's voice penetrated the darkness. Soft and low. "I did go down Wilson Lane. I sort of lost my way. And I was going along. Slowly. Very slowly. Trying to get my bearings. Slowly. Very slowly."

He paused and then went on. "There was a little accident. I did hit somebody."

"Alden."

"But nobody was hurt. Nobody."

"What?" Brad said. And he was now sure that there was someone standing under the tall elm tree.

Brad heard Alden's low and sincere voice. "Nobody. Believe me. I was going along slowly. You were asleep. Out cold. You were, old buddy. Believe me."

The dark, listening figure now silently slid behind the thick trunk of the elm tree and Brad could see it no more.

"Are you listening?" Alden said.

"I am, Alden."

"I was going along. Singing Yon Yonson. My arm around your shoulder. You don't remember that, do you?"

"No," Brad said.

"Just edging along the road. Half-asleep myself. And this fellow comes from out of the night. From nowhere." He paused again.

Brad waited.

Alden's voice lowered, almost to a whisper. "And he walks in front of the car. And I hit him."

Brad could see Alden's eyes in the darkness and there was a haunted look in them. And then the look was gone.

Alden's voice became firm and clear. "He wasn't hurt, Brad. He got up and I tried to talk to him but he just shook me off and walked away. Just turned and walked away. He had some drinks in him. I'm sure of that. A drifter."

"A road bum," Brad said quietly.

"Yes."

Brad thought of Ellen alone on the night beach, waiting for her father to come back.

"I guess he's alone in the world. Nobody but himself."

"Probably," Alden said.

Then there was a silence.

Brad finally spoke. "And you say he wasn't hurt?"

Alden nodded. "Not a mark on him. His clothes were dirty and dusty. But that's all. I was going too slow to hurt him."

"You're sure of that?"

"Positive."

Brad turned away from him.

Then he heard Alden's voice again. "I should have leveled with you from the beginning, Brad. I'm sorry I didn't. Maybe that's why I got so angry at you. Guilt feelings, old buddy. Guilt."

"For not leveling with me?" Brad murmured.

"Yes."

Brad looked to the tree. The shadow was gone. Only the black form of the tree remained. He turned to Alden.

"Have you talked this over with the Judge?" he asked.

"The Judge?"

"Yes, Alden."

Alden shook his head. "No. Why should I?"

"Why should you? You hit a person. A human being. Not a dog," Brad said.

"But—"

"Even a dog means something. If you hit a dog, you talk to somebody about it. You go and report it to the police."

"The police?"

"Yes, Alden."

"But he walked off. What was there to report?"

"He walked off," Brad murmured.

"Yes."

Brad looked coldly and silently at Alden.

Alden reached out and put his hand on Brad's arm. "What is it?"

Brad didn't speak.

"Tell me."

"You didn't level with me before," Brad said. "Are you leveling with me now?"

"I'm telling you the truth now."

"Should I believe you?"

"Why not?" Alden said.

Brad got up from the chair.

"Brad."

He stood there looking down at Alden. At the face pale in the darkness.

"I don't know what to believe," he said.

"Why?"

"I really don't. You never lied to me before, Alden. Never."

"And I'm not lying now. Do I have to swear it?"

"It won't help," Brad said.

Then he saw a stricken look come into Alden's eyes. And he felt a sharp pang within him. As if he had hit Alden. Hit him hard.

"Brad," Alden said in a shaky voice. "We're friends."

The look was still in his eyes. Still there. Brad could not bear it.

Alden spoke again. "We've been friends for a long, long time, old buddy. Did I ever let you down? Did I?"

Brad stood there in the vast stillness of the night. I'm caught, he thought bitterly. Caught.

"Brad?"

"We're friends," Brad said gently. Then he turned and walked away from Alden.

When Brad got into his car to drive off, he saw Mrs. Whitlock looking down from one of the upstairs windows. Looking down at him. Her face white and anxious. It seemed to him that her eyes were pleading with him.

I don't know what to believe, he said to himself. I don't. Then he started the car up and drove away into the darkness.

23

You believe what you want to believe. That's it. That's what everybody does. Every day of their lives. Why not me? Am I any different?

I want to believe what Alden just told me. In my heart of hearts I want to. Why shouldn't I? He's my friend. Old buddy. All through the years he was my best friend. Never once let me down. Never.

He even stood by me when I got into that stupid mess and was almost thrown out of school. He never wavered. Not once. Even got the Judge to use his influence to save me.

My father could do nothing. They had me nailed to the wall. Cheating on the finals.

I did it so I wouldn't be thrown off the track team. Stupid, stupid mess. And Alden got the Judge to save me.

You believe what you want to believe. And that's what I'm going to do.

Alden said the man wasn't hurt. He's ready to swear to it. That should be enough for me.

The man walked off into the night. Walked off unhurt. Alden was going too slow to hurt him. Too slow.

I believe Alden. That's what happened. Just as he says it did. Yes. And there's no more to be said or thought on the matter. No more. Why should there be? Why? You believe what you want to believe.

Brad drove steadily along the quiet road. He stared ahead into the broad moonlit night, a sense of peace beginning to settle over him, a sense of pure, serene release.

He breathed out low and relaxed in his seat. He hummed a song. It was Yon Yonson.

Suddenly, insidiously, the image of the gold watch crept into his consciousness. He saw again the watch lying quietly in his bureau drawer, its glint of cold light as he picked it up and held it in his trembling hand. He saw the dark stain on its faded ribbon, the stain that looked like a dried spot of blood. A damning spot.

Brad's hands tightened on the steering wheel. A desperate look of anguish came over his taut face.

I don't know what to believe, he said to himself bitterly. I don't.

24

He drove along the beach highway looking for Ellen. The moon had slid behind a huge bank of heavy clouds and now the night was vast and very dark. It made him feel more alone and lost.

I can't go home to that big empty house, he thought. I just can't. I want to see her and talk to her. Just to see that she's all right. Just that.

He passed a long stretch of empty, lonely beach and then he saw the dark hulk of her car. It gleamed faintly in the night. She had driven it off the highway and well onto the beach, not too far away from the murky, restless water.

Brad parked his car on the shoulder of the highway, turned off the lights, and then got out. The night was warm and oppressive. But as he walked along the sand to her car, he started to feel the breezes that came sweeping over the dark water and onto the beach. He came up to the car and peered within.

Then he heard the voice. Close behind him.

"Don't move."

It was her voice, low and harsh.

He was about to turn to her.

"Don't try it," she said. "Or I'll crack your skull."

"Ellen," he said.

He heard her gasp. "Brad?"

He turned and saw the gleam of a tire iron held in her hand, high over her head, ready to crash down on his.

"It's me," he said.

Her hand lowered to her side. "What are you doing here?" she said.

"Just wanted to see how you're making out."

"And you almost landed in a hospital. You know that?"

He nodded. "Yes, Ellen. I do."

"Or a morgue."

"You were going to come down hard."

"Hard as I could."

"I'm lucky you didn't."

"Very lucky."

She sighed gently. "You're a child, Brad. Nothing but a child."

"I guess I am."

She laughed. A soft laugh.

He smiled at her.

"Okay," she said. "You came to see how I'm making out. I'm doing fine."

He didn't speak.

"And I'm trying to get some sleep."

"You sleep like a cat," Brad said.

"A live cat. Have to. Or I'll end up a dead one." She laughed. He stood close to her but he could barely see her features in the dark. Yet he could feel her delicate body fragrance settle over him.

"You want me to go, Ellen?"

"Yes, Brad."

"I wanted to talk to you."

"We'll do that tomorrow. When we have lunch."

"Tomorrow seems like a long way off," he said.

"It'll get here. It always does."

"Just a little while?"

"No."

"Then I have to go?"

"You do."

"All right," he said in a low, disappointed voice.

He was about to turn away from her when she reached out her hand in the darkness and touched him.

"Brad," she said softly.

"Yes?"

"Come here."

He came close to her.

She put her arms about him and kissed him. Then she let him go.

"Tomorrow," she said.

"Ellen. Let me stay."

"No."

"Just a little while. Just that."

"I'll see you tomorrow."

She went into the car and closed the door. Then she turned up the windows.

He stood looking through the glass at her, desperately seeking her form. Still feeling her fragrance about him.

"Ellen," he whispered.

And then he turned and walked slowly, very slowly, over the soft sand to his parked car.

The kiss still on his lips.

25

He lay in bed and thought of Ellen, his eyes open, staring at the white ceiling, his hands clasped behind his head. He lay there, relaxed and easy. All other thoughts were gone.

He was alone in another world.

Alone and happy. Her arms about him and her lips kissing him softly. Ever so softly. He smiled.

She was never pretty, he said to himself. No. From the instant I saw her, she was beautiful. Her gray, direct eyes. And the way she smiles. Her whole face lights up when she does that. How did I ever think that she could be plain?

Impossible. No, I never thought that. Not even for an instant. She's beautiful. And everything about her is beautiful. He smiled to himself.

And slowly, gradually, his eyes began to close. The last thing he saw was her pale, fragile image. Slowly, slowly, fading away.

He whispered her name.
Ellen.
Ellen.
Ellen.
And he was asleep.

26

The phone rang and jerked him out of his sleep, as if a giant hand had reached out and grabbed him. He sat up, his eyes open wide.

He looked at the clock on the night table; it was one o'clock in the morning. Exactly. On the very second.

Brad picked up the receiver. "Hello?"

There was a silence.

"Hello?" he said again.

Again there was silence.

He was about to drop the receiver back onto its hook when he heard the voice. "Go to Winston's Body Shop."

"What?"

It was a muffled voice and he couldn't recognize it. "Go there."

A voice so blurred and strange he couldn't tell if it was a man's or a woman's.

"Who are you?" Brad said.

"Ask Tom about the Jaguar he repaired."

"Tom?"

"That's the name."

"Who are you?"

"Speak to Tom. Only to him."

"Who?"

"Ask him about the broken headlight," the voice said.

"Please tell me who you are."

But the voice went on relentlessly. "Ask about the blood that was on the headlight."

"Blood?"

"Yes."

Brad shivered in the darkness.

Then he heard the voice again. "You were in the car. I know that you were in the car. You are just as guilty as the driver if you do nothing about it. Go there."

And then the phone went dead.

27

Blood. The blood that was on the headlight. The broken headlight.

Ask Tom.

Tom.

The name hammered into his fevered consciousness, again and again, with a cruel, relentless rhythm, giving him no peace, unsettling his very being.

He felt it was getting hard to breathe in the narrow room. That the walls were closing in on him. Soon to crush him. He cried out low in terror.

Then, in a panic, he ran out of the bedroom, down the stairs, and out of the dark house. He stopped running when he reached the patio, his breath coming in low gasps. Brad stood there rigid, letting the night breezes stray over him, cooling his brow and rustling his hair.

"I've got to get hold of myself," he whispered. I've got to.

He grasped a chair tightly and then slowly sat down under the vast night sky. His face a small white blot in the immense darkness.

Brad sat there, hour after slow hour, his thoughts swirling about within him.

Who called me? Who could it be? I haven't a clue. Not a clue. Nothing. Absolutely nothing.

And yet something terrible is going on.

A coverup?

Could it be that?

Was the man killed? Is Alden lying to me? Could he kill a man and lie to me? Could he live with such a lie?

No. I mustn't think that. Or I'll go mad. I mustn't.

I've got to believe Alden. I've got to. For his sake. For mine. For Ellen's.

Why did I get into the car with him? Why?

Brad bowed his head and felt on the point of weeping. He jammed his fist to his lips. Just before morning it began to rain. Yet he didn't move. Just sat there asking the question over and over again.

The rain came down and drenched Brad.

Finally, he got up and went back into the dark, empty house with the rain lashing its windows. Lashing them with a cold fury.

He slept no more.

28

Brad found Winston's Body Shop at the end of a long, quiet street, just at the outskirts of the town.

He got out of the car, the morning sun in his eyes, and walked into a small, neat, but dingy office. The blinds were closed against the sun. The room was cool and shadowy.

A large, gray-haired man sat behind a small, cluttered desk. No one else was in the room.

The man looked up from some bills he was studying. He smiled pleasantly. "Can I help you?"

"Is Tom around?"

"No. I'm sorry," the man said.

"He in the garage?"

The man shook his head.

"Anywhere around? I'd like to talk to him," Brad said.

"Talk to me. Maybe I can help you."

Brad hesitated and then spoke. "It's about a car."

"Go on."

Brad hesitated and then spoke again. "It's about a Jaguar he repaired."

"Jaguar?"

"Yes."

The man still smiled but he took off his glasses and set them down on the desk, slowly, deliberately. His eyes quietly studied Brad.

"It's a friend of mine's car," Brad said. "He wanted me to speak to Tom about it."

"Oh."

"He can't get over here now. He hurt his leg. The car is stalling."

"I see." And the man smiled gently. But his eyes pierced into Brad.

"When was the car repaired?" he asked.

"Two or three days ago," Brad said.

"Are you sure?"

"Yes."

Then the man shook his head and spoke in a soft voice. "We haven't had a Jaguar in here for weeks."

"You haven't?"

"That's what I said."

The man slowly put his glasses on again and picked up one of the bills. He began examining the figures on it. Brad stood there awkwardly.

"Could I talk to Tom for a minute?" he said.

The man shook his head. "Tom's in New York. Picking up parts."

"When will he be back?"

"Not before the weekend."

The man reached for a wooden tray and dropped the bill into it. He glanced up. "Look, son," he said quietly, "you're in the wrong shop."

Brad didn't speak.

"Try Atlas. Over on Charles Street."

"Atlas?"

"Try them."

"Sorry I bothered you," Brad said.

The man smiled his pleasant smile again. "No bother. Come to think of it, there's a John who works for Atlas. You've probably got the names mixed up."

"I guess I have," Brad said.

"See John."

"Thanks."

Brad went out of the office and back to his car.

The man lied to me, he said to himself. I can feel it. He lied.

But why? Why?

Something terrible and brutal is going on.

A coverup.

The truth is being destroyed.

By a coverup.

And I'm caught in it.

Caught.

29

"I stopped over at number eight this morning. Spoke to the old man."

"And?"

Ellen shrugged. "My father didn't come back."

"Oh."

"But he will. I'm sure of that," she said.

"Are you?"

"Yes, Brad."

And then she looked away from him and was silent.

He won't come back, Ellen. I used to think that he would. Hoped it would be so. For your sake. For Alden's. For mine.

But now I know that he won't. I have no proof. None.

Only feelings that are deep in my bones. Feelings. No proof.

Yet I believe it as a certainty. He's never coming back, Ellen. Never.

Brad looked across the table at her and watched as she drank her coffee. The early afternoon sun made her hair glisten, gave her gray eyes a soft glow.

Then he heard her voice. "You've been very quiet, Brad," she said.

"Have I?"

"Yes. Hardly a word out of you."

"Didn't realize it."

"Well, I did."

He smiled at her. "I'm sorry, Ellen."

"Nothing to be sorry about. It's just that I like hearing you talk."

"Do you?"

"Uh-huh."

The waitress came over and dropped the check on the table, smiled, and walked away from them.

Ellen glanced at the check and then spoke again. "From the time I picked you up at the house you've said little or nothing."

"Had nothing much to say."

"No, Brad."

"I was just happy being with you."

She shook her head. "There's something inside of you wanting to come out. And you're not letting it."

He silently picked up the check and took out his wallet. She reached out and put her hand on his wallet.

"I said we were splitting the check, didn't I?"

"I have the money."

"Just take out half," she said. "Down the middle. The tip, too."

"Ellen."

114

"Do it, and give her twenty percent."

"I generally give fifteen. And everybody's happy." He shrugged. "Okay. Whatever you say."

"That's what I say."

"Do you always get your way?" Brad asked.

"Not always. But I've got a good batting average."

"I'll bet you do."

She laughed softly and then leaned forward to him. Her hand reached out to his. "What is it, Brad?" she asked gently.

"You mean what's bugging me?"

"Yes."

He sat there, feeling the tender warmth of her hand.

"Don't keep things in, Brad. Let them out."

"I don't know," he murmured.

"Tell me."

And within him, he said, if I tell her I could lose her. She would turn with anger on me. With bitterness. I would lose her. And I don't want that. I don't.

I feel so alone and lost now. I couldn't bear to lose her. I just couldn't.

"Brad?"

He looked at her gray, direct eyes and he felt that they could see right into him, to the very core of his being.

She could see. It was no use.

"Ellen," he said.

"Yes?"

"Let's get out of here. I . . . I feel kind of closed in."

"And?"

"Let's take a ride."

"Where to?"

He hesitated and then spoke. "Wilson Lane."

"Why there?" she asked.

115

"Just let's do it."

And it seemed to him that her face had paled.

"All right. Wilson Lane," she said. Her voice was low and quiet. As if she knew what was within him. Why they were going there.

The two rose and left the diner.

"Let me drive," he said.

She nodded silently.

30

Brad saw the tree and drove slowly, very slowly, until he came up to it and then he stopped the car. The day had turned gray.

Ellen sat silently at his side and waited for him to speak.

All along the lane neither one had said a word, each staring ahead into the sunless sky, like cold strangers.

The wide, grassy fields stretched almost endlessly about them. And now they had come to the bare, gnarled tree. Gnarled and alone. Brad stared at it.

Suddenly the night with all its horrors came rushing back to him. Overwhelming him. Brad closed his eyes for a bitter, fearful instant. An instant that seemed to him like an eternity.

Again he heard the scream of the cat. Piercing into him like a gleaming silver blade. Chilling his being, making him shiver all over. And then the night and the scream were gone. Only a well of silence remained. He opened his eyes and looked directly at the tree.

"Brad."

He still looked at the tree.

"Brad, what's wrong?" Ellen said.

Then as if in a trance, he put his hand into his pocket and took out the watch. He slowly turned to her.

"Ellen," he said in a hollow voice.

He held out the watch in the palm of his moist hand. It had a cold, dull gleam to it.

"Take it," he said.

She looked at him and then picked up the watch. Her eyes opened wide.

"Is it your father's?" he asked.

She slowly turned it over and read the initials engraved there. She gasped low. He saw her face become white and slack.

"It is your father's," he said.

She found her voice. "How did you get it?"

He pointed to the tall grass waving in the breeze. "I found it over there. The other night."

"Night?"

"Yes."

She looked down again at the watch.

"*P.M.H.* Paul Matthew Hanson," she said in a low voice and then she looked up fiercely to him. "It's here on the back of the watch. Here."

He didn't speak.

"You knew it belonged to my father and yet you never said a word to me."

"I didn't really know it. Not until—"

She cut in harshly. "Why didn't you tell me? Why?"

He didn't answer.

"You know more, don't you?"

"Ellen."

"Tell me. You know what happened to him. Tell me."

"I don't really know," he said in a low voice.

"You do, Brad. You must tell me."

She put her hand on his shoulder and he flung it off and got out of the car. The door slammed shut.

And it made him think of the slamming of the door on the night of the party. The slamming of the door, like the final sound of a prison cell door. Final and fatal. When he got into the car with Alden. Both drunk.

They rode away into the shining night, Alden singing Yon Yonson, rode away, happy. Oh, so happy. To end up at the tree. This dark, dark tree.

He heard her voice. "Brad."

"Let me alone, Ellen," he said. "Please."

He walked over to the tree and leaned against its bare trunk. He looked away from her and out over the broad fields to the distant gray horizon.

She still sat in the car. Motionless. The watch clasped in her hand. Her gray eyes full upon him.

Suddenly he began to speak.

"I don't know what happened, Ellen," he said in a low, weary voice. "I don't. You must believe me."

And then he went on, gazing out at the horizon, as if speaking to it and not to her. His face white and taut.

"I was drunk. Asleep. Someone else was driving the car," he said. "Driving it slowly. Very slowly." As he was talking he could almost hear Alden saying the words for him. "And a man came out of the night and walked in front of the car. And it hit him. Not hard. Not hard at all."

"My father?"

"It could have been. I don't know."

He had turned to face her.

"You do, Brad," she said.

"No, Ellen. All I know is that I found the watch in the grass. The night of the—" He paused and then went on. "No. It was the night after the accident. After it. That's when I found it." And he knew that in his distraught mind he had blended the two nights together. As if they were one and the same night.

She was silent.

His eyes pleaded with her. "The man wasn't hurt," he said. "Not at all. He walked off into the darkness. Didn't even want to speak. Just got up and walked off."

"Got up and walked off?"

"Yes."

"Unhurt?"

"Yes."

"How do you know that?" she asked.

He didn't speak.

"You say you were asleep," she said. "You couldn't have seen or heard anything."

"The driver swears that's what happened. Nobody was hurt. He was going too slow to—"

"That's what the driver says," she cut in.

"I've known him all my life."

"So you believe him."

"I do, Ellen."

"And he's a decent, honorable fellow, isn't he?"

He nodded silently.

"Wouldn't lie to you. Would he?"

She sat there in the car, looking coldly at him, her lips tight.

"That's what happened, Ellen. I swear to you that's what happened. Nobody was hurt."

She held up the watch. "There's blood on the ribbon," she said quietly. "Dried blood."

He paled.

"The last time I saw this watch," she said, "the ribbon was clean and neat. He was proud of this watch. Took better care of it than a lot of things. He cared more for this watch than for me. Always carried it in his breast pocket. Close to his heart, he used to say. There's blood on it, Brad."

He looked at her taut face and then he said to himself desperately, What's wrong with me? I came here to tell her everything. The doubts I have. The terrible, torturing doubts that are tearing me apart. To speak about the blood on the broken headlight. The phone call. The man in the body shop lying to me.

I came here to tell her. But I'm not doing that. Why?

Then he watched her get out of the car and walk toward him.

"Brad."

"Yes?"

"Why did you wait until now to show me the watch?"

He didn't answer her.

"Why?"

"I didn't know. I wasn't sure."

"You did know."

"No, Ellen."

"Why did you come back the night after the accident?"

"I don't know."

She shook her head. "You came back to search around here. Didn't you?"

"I don't know why."

"You do know."

"It's not that. It's. . . ." And his voice trailed away into silence.

She put her hand gently on his. "Brad, stop running away. Just hold still for a moment."

He looked up at her.

"You don't believe your friend, do you?" she said.

"Ellen, you're wrong."

"Am I?"

"Yes."

"You're still running."

"I'm not," Brad said.

"You are. Because inside of you, you don't believe him at all, Brad."

He was silent.

"And you can't face the truth. It's too much to handle."

"No, Ellen. It's not that at all."

"What then is it?"

"I . . . I can't explain it."

"You're still running," she said fiercely. "I should turn away from you and never see you or talk to you again."

"Ellen, please . . ."

"But I'm not doing that. Because we're going to get at the truth. And we're going to look hard at it. You and I."

She motioned to the car. "Get back in."

He slowly followed her to the car and got in beside her.

"I'll drive this time," she said.

Then she turned to him. "Did your friend notify the police?"

"No."

"That's what he told you," Ellen said. "I don't believe that. Let's go to the police station and ask some questions."

122

And then she drove off down the road, with him sitting silently beside her.

She began to speak again. "He gave a report. To protect himself. He was driving slowly. Alone. No one else was in the car. He told that to the police so they'd never come to question you. You get rattled too easily. You have a conscience. All they have to go on is his story."

"Ellen, you're . . ."

"Wrong? Just sit there with me and say nothing. I've come from Chicago to find my father. I'll show them the letter. You're my friend. Let me handle it. We'll get to the truth."

Truth? What is the truth? he asked himself desperately. And then he bowed his head.

31

What is truth? A great sage once asked. And then he ran off like a thief and didn't wait for an answer. I guess he knew there wasn't any answer. There never is one.

People look at things from so many different angles. Different perspectives. Like Alden. And the Judge. And me.

So many different versions of the truth. And there never is one version that holds up for everybody. I guess that old, wise philosopher knew that. That's why he ran. Because he knew that.

"Yes," Brad said in a low voice. "He knew that."

"What?" She had turned to him.

"I was thinking out loud."

"Well, stop it. Settle down," Ellen said.

He didn't speak.

"The police station is two lights down?" she asked.

"Yes. And then you turn right and go into the parking lot."

"Sit back and relax."

"Okay."

And they were silent again.

Before this is over I'm going to lose her, he said to himself. If I haven't lost her already. And I'm going to lose a lot more. Before this is over.

They drove along the main street of the town, the sky above them still gray and sullen, and then he heard himself speak again.

"Did you love your father?" he asked.

He wondered why he had said that to her. And then he realized that he had been thinking about Alden and his father, the Judge. And of his own father.

"You asked me that before, Brad."

"I did."

"And what did I answer?"

"I don't remember."

"Maybe this time I'll be giving you a different answer."

"Maybe you will, Ellen."

Truth shifts around, he thought to himself. It never stays put. It changes with time and place.

"Brad, I guess I can say that sometimes I did love him and sometimes I sure didn't."

"And when you didn't?"

"I despised him," she said.

He stared at her.

"No, Ellen."

"Yes," she said.

Then she nodded and went on speaking. "I despised him because he could be just plain rotten. And he was. I can't stand people who walk away from their responsibilities. No matter what happens you have to stay and hold on. If you love someone, you don't run away when things get tough."

"If you love someone," he said softly.

"That's the key to it all. I go in here?"

"Yes, Ellen."

She turned into the parking lot and then slid the car into an open space. She shut off the motor.

"You didn't ask me about my mother. Did you?" she asked.

"No."

"You should've. Because women count in this world, Brad. Count a lot. Even if you and a lot of guys like you think differently."

"I don't think differently, Ellen."

"You do. But let's not get into it."

He was silent.

"My mother held on until she could hold on no more," Ellen said. "She just gave up and died. I never stopped loving her. Not for an instant." She looked away from him and he thought her eyes had misted up.

Then she spoke again. "I'm like her. If I love somebody I stay with him. All the way. I haven't found that somebody yet. But I'm sure down the road I will."

"Down the road?"

"Uh-huh."

They sat there looking at each other. Then she stirred.

"Let's go in," she said.

"Okay, Ellen."

They got out of the car and she turned to him, her face cold and serious.

"Now listen to me, Brad," she said. "I'm going to ask them if my father's been in an accident on Wilson

Lane. And if he is in one of the hospitals around here. Let's see what they come up with."

Then she abruptly moved away from him and went into the building.

He slowly followed her.

I've lost her, he said to himself bleakly.

I know that now.

32

"Yes, your fears were right. There was a minor accident on Wilson Lane that night."

"Minor?" Ellen asked.

"It did involve your father. He was walking along
the road in the dark and he stepped in front of a
slow-moving car. But he wasn't hurt at all. Not at all."

"How do you know?"

"Because we questioned him."

"What?"

She stared at the police sergeant.

"We did, Miss Hanson. His exact words are here."

They were in a small, well-lit office, the sergeant
behind his neat desk, holding the accident report in
his hand.

"The car was moving too slowly to hurt him.
That's what he said."

A slender middle-aged man in a gray suit had

come into the room. He stood leaning against the now closed door, listening quietly, his lean face sharp and intent.

Brad sat next to Ellen, never speaking a word. But within him the doubts had begun again. The cruel, tearing doubts.

"Where did you question him? On Wilson Lane? That night?" Ellen asked.

The sergeant shook his head. "We only learned of the accident in the morning."

"And?"

"We immediately sent out a patrol car searching for your father. We found him on State Highway Forty-one trying to get a ride."

"Where was he heading?"

"He said to Pittsfield. Over the state line. For a job in one of the mills. He had heard about it and thought he'd take a shot at it. Those were his words."

"And you're sure it was him?"

"Paul Hanson. That is your father's name, isn't it?"

"Yes. It is. Who told you about the accident?"

"The driver of the car. Alden Whitlock."

"He came down here?"

The sergeant nodded. "With his father."

"The Judge came in with him?" The words broke out of Brad before he could stop them.

He saw the look of anger and despair in Ellen's eyes as she turned to him.

The man leaning against the closed door spoke quietly to Brad. "You know Judge Whitlock?" he asked.

Brad hesitated.

"Well, do you?" the man repeated.

Brad nodded. "Yes. Alden's my friend."

"And you are?"

"Brad Nelson."

The man smiled genially. "I'm Arthur Bailey, Chief of Police." He motioned to Ellen. "Don't let me interrupt, Miss Hanson. Go on with your questions."

Ellen turned back to the sergeant. "Was Alden Whitlock alone in the car? No one was with him?"

"No one."

"That's what he told you?"

"Yes."

"Have you any doubts, Miss Hanson?" the police chief asked gently.

Ellen looked calmly over to him and shook her head. "Just asking," she said.

"Please go on."

She spoke again to the sergeant. "You're sure that was my father you found on the highway?"

"Yes. He had identification on him. Positive identification."

"Had he been drinking?"

"Drinking?"

"He has that problem."

The sergeant smiled. "Well, I would say he had a bit in him. Just a bit. Not too much."

Ellen smiled.

"Then he would have shown you his watch. It comes from Civil War days. Handed down until my father got it. He was always very proud of it. And when he was a little high he'd take it out and show it to anybody around. He had his initials put on it."

"A watch, you say?"

"A small gold watch. He said it was in the Battle of Bull Run." The smile was no longer on her face.

The sergeant glanced over to the chief.

The man spoke. "Yes. It was on him. It should be there in your report, Sergeant."

130

The sergeant studied the report, turned a page and then nodded. "It's here."

The chief spoke again.

"Mr. Hanson was asked if he wanted to press any charges against Alden Whitlock."

"And?"

"He refused. He said he just wanted to get going."

"He told you that?"

The chief nodded. "Those were his exact words. I read them in the report given to me."

He came over to Ellen and smiled gently at her. "You must wonder why I'm here now. When I was told that you had come all the way from Chicago to meet your father and didn't find him, I became concerned."

"That's kind of you," Ellen said.

"The least I could do. Now if you want me to get in touch with the Pittsfield Police, please tell me."

"I'd appreciate it."

"Where can I contact you?" he asked.

"I'll be staying around for a day or two. So I'll drop in again."

"Fine."

She got up. "Thanks very much for all you've done," she said. "It's good knowing that my father is still in good shape. I was worried."

"He's in good shape and good spirits," the sergeant said.

Ellen laughed softly. And then she went out of the office followed by Brad. Leaving the two men alone. Their shadows long on the bare walls of the room.

33

All the way back to his house Ellen didn't say a word to him. Just sat in her seat, her eyes staring straight ahead, cold and glinting, her lips tight.

She drove the car into the driveway and stopped but didn't turn off the motor.

"He's never coming back," she said. Her voice was low and flat. Her face pale, so very pale.

Brad didn't speak.

"You knew that. Knew it all along, didn't you?" she said.

"Ellen, I—" His voice trailed away into silence.

"Tell me. You knew it."

Brad slowly nodded.

Her eyes flashed bitterly at him. "He's dead. You sat in a car and saw him killed and you never said a mumbling word to anybody. Not one word."

"No, Ellen. I saw nothing."

"Liar."

"It's the truth."

"What is truth to you, you liar? You're lying just as they are lying. You're just like them, Brad. They have no conscience and you have no conscience. None. Do you hear me? None. And I cared for you. Truly cared for you." Her voice broke.

"Ellen," he murmured.

But she turned away from him and started crying softly.

He sat there, his heart breaking for her. He wanted to reach out and hold her close to him. To comfort her.

But she began to speak again. This time there was cold fury in her voice. "Killed him. Killed him and got rid of the body. Like a sack of garbage. Why not? A homeless bum on the road. What did he amount to? What? Next to that rich, spoiled friend of yours and his father, the powerful judge? They count in this screwed-up, hypocritical world of ours. They sure do. And he? Paul Hanson? A useless nothing. Waste material. Throw him away. Just throw him away."

Her hand, closed into a fist, beat down on the steering wheel.

Once.

Again.

And then it opened and fell away.

She bowed her head.

When she spoke again, her voice was low and almost futile. "And there is nothing I can do about it," she said. "Because everybody will deny, hand on a Bible, deny and deny. A wall of denials. Nothing I can do."

"I won't let them get away with it," Brad said fiercely. "I won't, Ellen."

She turned to him, the tears still in her eyes. "I said you were a child. And you now talk like a child. You'll do nothing. They hold all the cards. All of them."

And then she went on. "This is a setup. Anybody who goes up against them will be framed and land in jail. I saw this happen in Chicago. Why can't it happen here? It's a coverup. A stinking, rotten coverup."

"I don't care. I won't let them—"

She cut in coldly. "Listen to me. No matter what you say you want to do now, you were part of a killing. You were."

"No, Ellen."

"You sure were. Because you never said a word. Not a mumbling word. You sat still and let it go on."

He was silent.

Her voice rose in bitterness when she spoke again. "You're a good and decent person. And yet how different are you from the good and decent Germans who knew about the concentration camps and said and did nothing about them? And the good and decent Americans who learned about the massacre of men, women, and children at My Lai and kept their mouths shut! What difference is there between them and the good and decent person who sees a hit-and-run accident and walks away from it because he doesn't want to get involved? Tell me. What difference?"

"You don't understand," he said.

She shook her head fiercely. "There's nothing to understand. Listen to me. If you start anything, they'll end up proving that you drove the car. Not your friend, but you. You. You drove it while you were stinking drunk."

"They can't do that."

"Can't they? Listen, you fool. They'll simply make up another phony accident report. Can you prove that you didn't drive the car? Can you? Did anyone see your dear friend drive it that night down Wilson Lane? Well, did anyone?"

He didn't answer.

"They hold all the cards. All of them. And they're all aces." Her voice faded away bitterly.

The two sat silent under the bleak, gray sky.

Brad thought of Alden. And he found himself hating him. Hating him for what he had done. And was doing.

Then he heard Ellen speak. "The Judge. He must be a real powerful man in this community. This stinking, corrupt community."

Her hands clenched and then unclenched futilely. A poignant, haunted look came into her eyes. Haunted and defeated.

"Brad," she said.

"Yes."

"I guess I'll head back for home. Now."

"No, Ellen."

"Go back and forget it all. I got along without him while he was alive and I'll get along with him dead."

"Please don't go, Ellen."

She shook her head. "There's no reason for me to stay. There's nothing I can do."

"There must be."

"Nothing." And her voice hardened. "But I'll never forget what your friends did. Never."

Nor what I did, he thought bleakly.

He looked at her grim face and then slowly got out of the car.

She sat there, her gray eyes full upon him.

135

He knew that as long as he lived he would never forget the deep, sad look that was in them. Never.

"Good-bye, Brad," she said gently.

And then he watched her drive off.

"Good-bye, Ellen," he said.

But she was too far away to hear him.

34

Brad sat around brooding the rest of the day. At nightfall he got into his car and drove along the beach highway looking for her, looking desperately, hoping against hope that she was still there, that she had not gone back home. But all he saw was desolate beach and dark, dark water.

He got out of the car and walked along the sand to the exact spot where her car had been parked. But there was no sign of Ellen. Or of the car. The wind and the sand had drifted over the spot, taking it back, as if she had never been there. Never held him in her arms and kissed him. Never.

He stood there, a lone and forlorn figure against the night.

I just wanted to see her, he said to himself. Just that. To talk to her again. To hear the sound of her voice. Just that. Just that and no more.

I shouldn't have let her go away without . . . Without what? What's the difference?

She's gone.

Forever gone.

Somewhere down the road she'll meet someone she'll love. Down the road.

He slowly turned and went back to his car. He was about to put the key into the ignition when her words came back to him. With a savage force.

"I'll never forget what your friends did. Never."

I won't either, Alden.

Then he drove along the highway, the soft thunder of the waves in his ears.

Drove to see Alden.

His face white and grim.

35

He found Alden sitting alone beside the dark tennis court, his long legs stretched out in front of him. His racket lay on the ground beside the chair.

"Hello, old buddy," Alden said quietly, as if he had been expecting him.

Brad sat down beside him.

"You didn't bring your racket."

"No, Alden. I didn't."

"Just came to talk."

"To talk." He was surprised how calm his voice sounded.

Alden picked up a white towel and wiped his face and then his brow. Carefully. Deliberately. Then he draped the towel about his neck.

"I heard you were at the police station, Brad," he said.

"I thought you would."

"You should leave it alone, old buddy. Leave it alone."

"Yes, Alden. I should."

"Our lives are ahead of us. You know that."

"I do."

"Where is your girlfriend? I was sure she'd be here with you."

"She went back to Chicago, Alden."

"Oh?"

"She gave up and went back."

"I guess she understood."

"She understood."

"That there are things that get beyond our control."

"They do, Alden. They sure do. When we let them."

And he looked toward the cluster of trees and he thought he saw a figure standing by the tall elm. Standing and listening. Just as he had seen a figure the other night. But this time he couldn't make out who it was. Darkness shrouded the form. He heard Alden's voice. "Something happens and there's nothing we can do about it, Brad. Nothing."

"Like murder, Alden?"

The clouds in the dark sky shifted and a spill of moonlight fell on the two of them, cold, cold moonlight, and Brad could see a haunted gleam come into Alden's eyes. And he knew that he had reached deep into the core of his friend's being.

"Murder?" Alden's voice trembled.

Brad rose from his seat. "That's what I said."

"What are you talking about?"

"You killed that man, Alden. Hit him with your car. And then you went running to the Judge for help. And he helped you all right. He sure did, Alden."

"Bradley."

140

The voice cut through the darkness like a knife.

Brad turned and saw the tall, solid figure of Judge Whitlock come out of the night and over to him.

"Don't come here talking of murder. Do you hear me?"

The Judge's face was taut with anger.

Brad didn't speak.

"You were told the man is alive and well. And he is."

"That's not so," Brad said.

"That is so. And that is what the record states."

"It's a lie."

"No. The truth."

"I won't let you get away with it," Brad said.

"Don't cross me," the Judge said. "Or you'll live to regret it. Regret it bitterly."

"I don't care what you say, I'm going to—"

And suddenly the lights of the court were switched on and he stopped speaking. They all turned and saw the silent, grim figure of Mrs. Whitlock. She stood there facing them, her face cold and white.

"Emily," the Judge said.

There was a chilling silence.

And then she spoke. "You're not getting away with this, Peter," she said in a low, cold voice. "Not this time."

Judge Whitlock paled.

"Emily, stay out of this."

She shook her head fiercely. "I'm in. And there's nothing you can do about it. Nothing."

He suddenly shouted. "Emily, do you think I'm going to let Alden's life be wrecked by a drunk walking along a road at night? A wretched, miserable drunk? To have his career shattered by a staggering drunk? Do you?"

"You're not saving Alden's life, you fool," she said. "You're wrecking it. Forever. Tell him, Alden."

Alden looked to his mother and bowed his head. He put his hand to his face.

She came over to him. "You can't have that on your conscience, Alden. You can't do that and live. It will destroy you." She put her arm around her son.

"Emily," the Judge shouted.

She looked over to him and shook her head. "No, Peter."

"I'm going to stop you. Right now."

"Let it alone, Father," Alden said in a broken voice. "Let it alone."

"No. Alden, don't listen to her."

"He has to, Peter. And there's nothing you can do to stop me. It's too late. I've already talked to the governor."

"What?" he whispered.

"It's all going to come out in the open. It's too late for you to do anything, Peter."

The Judge stared at her and didn't speak.

"Too late," she said. "I talked to the man who repaired the car. He will testify that there was blood on the headlights. Too late, Peter. For you. But not for Alden. He can still be . . ."

Her voice choked up for an instant. Then her lips tightened into a firm line and she turned to Brad. "It was I who called you, Brad. I was too weak and confused to do anything. I wanted you to go on and . . . I found I couldn't stand silent anymore."

"Emily," the Judge said in a low and dead voice.

"Go home, Brad. This is now between us."

Brad looked at her and he saw the tears in her eyes, and then he walked away, leaving the figures alone under the dark night.

36

He sat on a bench under a tree, on the college campus in Chicago.

The day was bright and cold. Autumn had come in.

He sat there and thought of Alden and his father.

Alden was now in prison. His father had just barely escaped a sentence, but his political power was smashed. He would never be the same again.

The police force had been shaken up from top to bottom.

Brad had gone with Mrs. Whitlock to visit Alden.

But the Judge would never forgive him.

"How could you live with your conscience, Bradley? How?"

He sat there thinking of the Whitlocks.

And then of his own mother and father.

He had sat between them when Alden was sentenced to two years in prison. He remembered the tears that came to his eyes as he looked across the room to Alden. Brad had bowed his head and his father had put his arm about him silently. His mother had said softly, "Brad." That was all.

Now he sat there on the bench under the leafless trees still hearing her tender voice.

"Brad."

Suddenly he trembled.

"Brad."

He couldn't move.

He looked up.

There was Ellen's face, looking down at him.

"It's good to see you," she said.

He nodded silently.

Is this what happens to the heart? he thought.

You just give it away?

All away?

She slowly sat down next to him.

"I've just registered," he said. And his voice sounded distant and hollow.

"Then we'll be together a long time," she said.

"Yes."

And suddenly she was in his arms.

Under the bright autumn sun.